D o g R

TATIANA STRAUSS

Other Books By The Author

Pussy Willow

Blue Speedwell

Cover photograph by Maria Matheou

Visit www.tatianastrauss.com to find out more about the
author. You will also find news of any author
events and you can sign up for e-newsletters so that
you are always first to hear about new releases

Follow Tatiana on Instagram: tatiana_strauss_author

Acknowledgments

My loving appreciation and thanks to Sarah for your eternal friendship, play, belief in my human expression and your limitless love. So many thank yous, Maria, for your love, your contributions, for your constancy, fun and so much more. To Mandi, to GlenRay, to Amelia, thank you for being all that you are in my life. To Katharine, and Nicci too, you who came along later to walk the walk with me. To every friend who cheered and supported me and read me along the way, my heartfelt thank you. Thank you dearly to Barry, who saluted me in everything I am, who was here from the beginning of my path as a writer—and so many more beginnings—you mysteriously took off—god, that hurt—and god, I've grown—but you're always here and your mark is forever in my life and in my work. Thank you to my mama, who was the maker of my own human beginning. To my papa. And my siblings—to Vanessa in particular, for you know why. My thanks to Jean McNeal and Giles Foden for encouraging me in the early days of the novel which was to become this series. To UEA. To John Boyne and Henry Sutton. To Ivan Mulcahy. To Broo Doherty. Thank you to Kosta Ouzas, Tamsyn Bester, Alex and the team at SPH. Thanks to Henry Glover. To Grace Mattingly.

To Dani Zargel. A huge thank you for the teachings and inspirations of the Buddha and the many teachers thereof; to Abraham Hicks for inspiring me via your extensive YouTube presence and teachings, also for your book, *Ask and it is Given*; to Eckhart Tolle for *The Power of Now*; to Anita Moorjani for sharing your NDE in interviews about your book, *Dying to be Me*. Thank you to Aaron Abke for your extraordinary gift of articulating a myriad spiritual teachings, and for resonating into my life in the last moments of my final edit of this book. Thank you to all and everyone who inspired me—on purpose or otherwise—who supported me; who led me to grow by shadow or by light; to all those I have loved, still love, and those who loved me or love me still…appreciation lives in me for you all.

DogRose

Ragged Robin

It was the strangest, most amazing sensation, made me kind of blurry inside, as if I wasn't really me anymore; didn't even know what me meant. My whole outline was inflaming, my insides too, all swelling right out of my lips. I felt I might be some kind of puff adder, zigzags bloated-as and warning you off—or calling you maybe, for your crazy curiosity—yes, calling you in, and biting you, showing you somewhere deeper than you ever knew, like maybe you were beyond material, just pure tingling energy, all super-conscious. I felt my tongue like that snake's, flicking around in the boy's mouth on its own, tasting him, pushing at, playing with, his tongue, and my lips felt just about like they were eating him. Which was almost, could have been, horrible, but was actually sort of exciting. And anyway, my lips were doing this without me—so I felt maybe all of me actually, *really* began from my swollen kiss.

I realised I was melting, all sort of molten, very hot and in motion,

1

my whole field red and spangly beneath my fluttery closed lids. I wasn't an adder anymore; *oh no!* I was lava spurting out of a volcano, I could see myself flowing and whizzing in scorching scarlet orange yellow black rivers all over the place, devastating the strandy pink-petaled ragged robin flowers on the mountain. When a frond of my long dark hair snagged in his fingers, I took in he was sliding his hand about me, over my grey V-neck school jersey, around my waist, over my ribs and up to my small right boob—somewhere in me said I should stop him, because that's what you were supposed to do, but the whole thing was so glorious and new, I just didn't care to. I wanted to know.

This was for me, see. This kid barely existed as a person in my mind—I didn't even really like him—or I just a bit *liked* him—or maybe someone else, maybe—more like—I mean really, this was just some stupid boy, a bit kind of stale-smelling, with his dumb mustard-and-black striped school tie made squat and fat below his unbuttoned collar. Pretty soon he was going to get told off by some teacher and made to do up his top button and he would blush and bristle, have to do it anyway. He would flash his muddy-brown eyes, wobble his straggling curly head, try to look tough, and it would be pathetic.

My mouth still dancing with his, I felt just a little bit like a hypocrite, while at the same time I felt myself a winner. I found myself smiling, an extra little clicky sound coming soft through the popping star-burst orchestra we were already producing. I thought of Space Dust, the little black envelope of a packet kiddiewink-you ripped the top off of, tangy orange crystals you put in your mouth for their madcap abstract explosions. All kinds of sweet delights came tripping onto my tongue: Curly Wurly, its chocolate-covered caramel in the shape of DNA; Nutty bar, all walled in toffee and peanuts; *oh!* Flake—singing, *Only the crumbliest, flakiest*—and then his fingers were squeezing my boob, quite hard, so it hurt, and I felt an urge to smack him off; immediately felt a fresh scud of heat.

'You like it?' he said, breath sort of sour into my mouth.

My lips reached and sucked his back. I had the impression he was looking at me, at my mashed-up soft-focused face, at our slippy lips maybe, as they were kissing. I felt the tickle of his bumfluff above his upper lip, all kind of tender, like a tiny bird with maybe a red breast had landed there. My own eyes stayed clamped shut, and I let familiar ripples flood into my pelvis, felt myself to be cantering on one of the racehorses at my uncle's work, all when he was still in Suffolk and I used to be there all the time, just a bike-ride away from us, before he got poached by those fancy French people in Ireland. I heard a smudgy moan come out of my throat; heard him kind of groan, his fingers slicing a chilly crack between sweater and skirt. His palm against my skin was clammy. It stuck to me in a sort of shambolic staccato. My dear tiny robin flew off and thoughts of what a smelly cringe *this* boy was went crashing through the burn of me— but he hit my silky bra, everything going smooth again, and it just didn't matter who he was or I was or what he smelled like or anything. The tingles rushed me, secret openings that were mine, and mine alone.

A noise came sharp, something outside of us: the shove and suck of the door, of a body pushing at its dense weight. Our reflexes were quick; we sprang apart as if we were struck. He darted into the cubicle behind him, whilst I rested my bum back into the chill rim of the small white hand-basin I had been leaning against, worked hard to relax my outer form—inner body yet smiling, flying, in a kind of delightful chaos. Some girl from the sixth form, a Prefect of course, came from behind the fireproof veneer, letting it swing shut behind her and, I saw, flashed in my mind—or maybe really saw, I'm not sure it

3

was possible—the smear of her handprint on the morning shined brass push-plate screwed to the door's exterior. I saw something vital and beautiful, transient; a trace of life soon to be wiped out.

She paused, gave me a long, too long, look. She was kind of small, way shorter than me, with hair falling in soft pretty waves to her slim broad shoulders, hair even darker than mine, looked properly black. A leather band, with a few studs in it, rung around her throat, and she was squeezed into the most skintight pale-grey cords I'd ever seen.

I fiddled in my skirt pocket, drew out a dinky glass vial of roll-on cherry lipgloss, ambled it over my lips, all the time eyeing her. 'I'm not a book, you know,' I told her.

'What?'

'That you can read.'

She laughed in a single breath, through her nose, her large black eyes going all hooded and penetrating. She stared at me quite a while, with a look of triumph. My insides were still making endless echoes I hoped weren't flushing up into my face. 'Hmmm,' she said. 'You think?'

'True,' I said.

Her smile softened and her eyebrows shot up. She shook her head, real slow. Again, she waited for some time, eyeballing me while I screwed the cap onto my lipgloss, returned it to my pocket. Then she indicated the locked toilet cubicle, gave me a knowing look, pulled in her mouth, made a stifled viscous laugh.

I held her stare, surprised as a similar sound came out of me. The feeling in my body now related to her, waves rushing at my chest. I didn't know if I was scared or excited. I bit on my smile, teeth into my lower lip, shrugged.

Her forefinger raising to her lips, she made a silent shh-y shape. I found this sort of pretty, somehow alluring. She indicated the door again, seemed to be checking with me for permission. I gave her a stiff little nod. She took several clattering steps to the closed cubicle door. Her fisted hand came up, tapped quite lightly on the grey-speckled Formica.

'Cleaner,' she announced to the door, tone all strident and authoritative, bright eyes flicking back to me and keeping mine captive. She held out her loose fist and rhythmically opened each finger, mouthing: one, two, three, four, five, six; and then just the fingers and a growing grin, tongue showing between her slightly crooked teeth, as she increased her emphasis with her shooting digits, finishing up to ten.

I stayed myself with a smile, leaning against the basin. I became aware of a rich crescent of dampness pressing through my skirt along the sink-line and cutting quite pleasantly into the upper cheeks of my bottom. A small shudder went through me, along with it, a new thrill at our unfolding cruelty.

'Hello?' she sung out. 'You alright in there, love?'

She nodded at me as a kind of prompt, and I piped, 'You okay?'

My shoulders jumped with cheek at my next thought: 'Darlene?' A wicked energy rose between the sixth-former and I. Mutual moisture sprang from under our lids, sheened us, cemented us in union. I didn't know if I could control the turncoat laugh that wanted to break. '*Darlene*?' I said again, clamping my palm over my mouth.

'Darlene dear? You're starting to worry us, love. You better come out, dear old thing.'

To the cleaner, I said, 'She's not very well, see? I think she was going to puke. Only now I'm worried she's dead, huh?'

'Oh...well, no doubt she's alive—and kicking—but we better get Darlene to the nurse. Has she seen the nurse?'

'Um—no. I don't think she wants to. It's a very—*personal*—problem,

5

see.'

'Ah. Her period?'

I nodded, silent laughter radiating out of me.

'I see. First time?'

'Yeh,' I croaked.

'Have you had yours yet?' she asked me.

I shrugged, nodded, grinned.

'Darlene dear, there's really nothing to be ashamed of. It's very normal. You'll be fine, love. The human body has buckets of blood. Buckets.'

'Maybe...' I said, all stabbed with some kind of guilt and pointing out the vending machine on the wall by the door. 'Maybe we should just slip her a panty pad and leave her to it? Let her maintain her dignity? Don't you think?'

The Prefect made a wry face. 'Well, *maybe*. But I do need to hear from her, ascertain she's alright first. Darlene, love. Please answer me and tell me you can manage, dear. I do have an Allen key to unlock the door from out here, and if you don't speak with me right now...I'm sorry, but I shall have to consider this an emergency and make use of it. You understand? However, I don't want to find you all bloody on the loo.'

A high-pitched shriek from behind the Formica said, 'Yes. I'm fine.'

'Are you bleeding heavily?'

'Hmmm...'

'Have you seen *Carrie*?'

'Er...what?'

'The movie, Darlene. *Carrie*. All that blood they dump on her head at the prom, it's pig's blood, *Jo*lene, huh? It's only representative of menstrual blood, nothing to worry about.'

The laugh in my throat sort of fizzled out, a tightness running down the back of my neck. I fumbled in my skirt pockets, fished out some change, held it out. 'Shall-shall I...get the—er—shall I?' I made a move toward the vending machine. 'And then we can get out of here and leave her—'

'—I don't think *he'll* need it. Do you?' The girl's expression changed as she stared at me, tapped at her yellow Prefect's badge the shape of a shield. She leaned with one shoulder into the toilet door, all the while her gaze on me, just a flick of her eyes indicating him, as she said, 'And you, Jolene dear? What do *you* think?' She allowed a space for his answer, still with her eyes haunting me. I saw her chest rise up. Her gaze dropped down my body, back up again. To me, she said, 'Shouldn't you be in class? You could get into a lot of trouble for this, you know. I could get you in a lot of trouble.'

I shrugged, forced a smile, wondered, had she been playing with me—the cow—and now she was going to tell on us.

'I'm not going to tell on you, if that's what you're thinking. Book girl.' To the Formica door, she said, 'You better come out, boy. For your information I saw you. And I know what you were doing in here too, you two.'

'What are you?' I said.

'Me?'

'Yep, you.'

'*What?*—you say? I might be your nemesis, huh? Or I might be your ally. Take your pick, girl. Is he your boyfriend, that one?' She grazed her eyes across the flimsy door.

I shrugged. I didn't want to tell her he wasn't. Even though I wanted so much to tell her, of course not, are you mad? I wasn't sure I wanted to give her anything.

'I   would   venture   to   say...'   I   said   '...maybe...perhaps,

7

*actually…*you're a psycho.'

She chuckled, went all lit up and soft again. 'Venture eh? Would you?'

'I would. I'm *ad*venturous, see.'

'Ah…*ad*venturous book girl.' She shook her head, turned her frame to face me full-on, arms folded, let her back rest into the speckledy-grey. 'Nah. I'm not. A psycho.' And quite lightly, she murmured, all gazing at me, 'Come on, boy, time's up.'

'Just come out,' I said.

'I'll give you another ten seconds. Or else I'm sending you to the Head. Come on.'

We heard the swish of movement from within. The Prefect pushed herself clear of the door. I knew she watched me askance, but I wouldn't look at her. He cleared his throat. And the latch slid back. I watched it, feeling her watching me. He pulled the door open, stood looking from she to me and back again. I noted how dishevelled he was, his white shirt all half-out of his trousers, his hair kind of greasy, one of his shoelaces undone, frayed and licking the mottled floor. I turned my eyes to the girl's, handed her a tremendous smile.

Clearly satisfied, she gave her attention to the thing in the doorway. 'Ta-da,' she growled. 'It lives.'

He looked to me for some kind of support. I shrugged one shoulder. 'I didn't do anything wrong,' he said.

'No, like being in the girls' toilets isn't something wrong, huh? And skipping class isn't something wrong. Let alone what the fuck you might have been up to with—' she indicated me '—this one.'

My eyes fell, licked the floor tiles, along with his shoelace, right as he barked, 'You can't speak to me like that.'

'Oh no? Try me. You fancy a picnic in the Headmaster's office, be my guest.'

8

He grunted. He might have been good looking, but I saw him, in that moment, as kind of pretty ugly. The traces of acne on his cheeks made a jigsaw with that dumb fluffy moustache.

'Just get the fuck out of here,' the Prefect told him.

Stepping around her to leave, he muttered something calculated to be inaudible. 'I heard that.' She yanked him by the upper arm, twisted him into her with marked force. He towered over her. 'Fuck you too.' And she released him, shoving him as if he was filthy.

He sort of stumbled backwards toward the exit, grabbed a hold of the brass door handle, made eye contact with me. 'And fuck *you*.'

'He wishes,' said the girl.

I lost it then: just broke into a fit of wild laughter. I saw how the Prefect smiled wide, looking all pleased with herself.

'You're a traitor,' the boy hissed at me. 'And a slag.' To her, he said, 'I would've too, if you hadn't barged in. She was well up for it.'

My laughter just went like space dust—me, all shaking my head and tears pouring out and dark shards of hair falling all into my face. It was such a sensational feeling, like all my nerve endings were electric and every cell was a tiny bomb exploding throughout my body. The boy, he looked furious. And under the fury, he looked wounded; the way small sparks went off in his face, I could tell.

And suddenly I remembered I kind of liked him and that he had liked me really a lot, it had been clear from the way he looked at me in the corridors between lessons and at break times. I thought how he had stepped in and saved me, though he wouldn't have seen it this way—but he had—from all the hurt and poison I had been made to ingest from the horrible stupid stuff Robin Remick had said about me, unbelievable stuff, after we had wound up in my friend's double bed together, when a gang of us had stayed over at her dad's weekend country cottage, less than a week ago, all of us sleeping in her room.

We had done this thing I could never have known about, while everyone else was asleep, awakening me to the most unimagined ecstasy. The wonders of that night had been smashed to bits by him. I just couldn't understand it. And when I learned he'd spread rumours about me, lies, my anger had masked the sharpest pain. All these thoughts and memories raked through me in a second, and, looking at the boy, I felt my stomach turn, felt the sting of bile, but I just kept on laughing. I laughed him out of the Yellow House girls' toilets and when I glanced at the Prefect, I saw how her expression had gone kind of dark and half-serious in the smile she wore and I felt like she was reading me again. I wanted to tell her to get lost and leave me to myself.

She clicked her tongue. 'Maybe *you're* the psycho.'

'Maybe. So? Takes one to know one.'

She shook her head, slipped her thumb beneath the band at her throat so the leather went all taught, all undulating atop her digit which went sliding back and forth. 'That doesn't sound like you.'

'And?'

'That kind of yokel talk.'

'That's a bit rude, isn't it? "Yokel".'

She puckered her lips, blew a laugh. I sensed some kind of shyness in her, beneath her tough act. I felt suddenly grateful. I liked the way she glowed—in it, the way she seemed to like me. We gazed at each other, all soft and smiling easily.

'What year are you in?' she asked.

I shrugged. 'Does it matter?'

'Um—' she pulled down one side of her plump little mouth '—just curious. I don't recall seeing you about.' I wanted to tell her I was new and in the sixth form, like her. But I figured it was a bad idea. I opened my mouth, was about to come clean, when she cut in, 'Do

10

you want to meet up after school? I've got to get to the Art department now—Mr Milton is waiting for me—' she indicated the toilet cubicle adjacent to the recently vacated one '—after I take a pee.'

Calibrating to this pretty thrilling prospect, I said, all casual, 'Yeh, sure. But I can't tonight. Maybe better to meet in town on Saturday? I live quite a bit away and have to get home on the school bus, see.'

'Got'cha…how about meeting at the bike sheds at dinnertime?'

'This dinnertime?'

'You don't want to?'

'No…I mean, yes…just I might have plans already this dinnertime. Tomorrow?'

She made that smile of hers, one side only. 'Sure. Tomorrow.'

'Okay.'

'You sure you can make that, in your busy schoolgirl schedule?'

Breaking the intensity of her gaze, I swivelled myself off of the basin rim, stared at myself in the mirror. I pretended to find wiping lipgloss from the corners of my mouth absorbing. I could feel her all watching me in the glass. Staring into my own pale-grey eyes, I said,

'Don't you sometimes wish you were Alice and you could just go right through the looking-glass into another reality?'

'I *am* Alice. In Wonderland. My wonderland. Maybe you are too, huh?'

Every Yellow Flower and a Dog Rose

Me and Katie Tippin and Jim Clarke and Jason Wallington, along with that gingery Paul someone-or-other from the upper sixth who really looked like a man already, all hairy and massive—had my mum swooning over him, embarrassing herself, when he spoke with her—we all of us disgorged from the school coach with the keen velocity of popcorn popping itself from a hot pan. I paused on the road, glanced back up to wave at the driver, intending to gratify one of my obsessions and get a glimpse of his glass eye, by accident arresting the progress of a couple of newbie younger kids who were about to descend back to earth, grinned at them in a way I hoped was scary, just because, then stepped aside, only to get an eyeful of Robin Remick as he mooched, all full of himself, off the high step, about crashing into me. It felt deliberate. And it felt mean. He didn't look at me, just made out like I wasn't hardly there and veered off up the road in the direction of his home.

I felt the rush of scarlet up my cheeks. I wanted to race after him, for everything to be like normal again, for us to natter and nudge and muck about together. I got the impression as I stared after him, he too, was cherry, and I wondered why he hadn't gotten off at the second stop the other end of our village, as he had recently taken to doing. My heart thumped in my throat, felt massive, like a caged miniature boxer trying to get out, and then it betrayed me, turned into an opera singer singing his name all inside of me. I always liked the way he flushed up through the tawny brown of his baby-smooth skin when he got excited. A sting of tears flicked at my eyes—but I refused them—turned myself onto the grassy knoll which made a V between the roads, let the downward momentum of the hillock whizz me over the crunch of chippings, across the grippy black tarmac, leap me over the curb stone, onto the opposite pavement. I sped alongside the village green, became aware of the ice cream van parked there, changed direction toward it.

'One raspberry Mivvi, please,' I said, scattering some silver change onto the counter.

Jim Clarke came up behind me, reached his arm past me, snapped a fifty pee in amongst my coins. 'Make that two.' He winked at me, a look of concern coming into his face. 'You, okay?' He was a curious fellow, very small and slight, with a silky golden-brown pudding-basin haircut and eyes like little blue fishes. His white skin was a sorry rash of pustules. 'He say anything to you?'

My fingertips gripped the cool metal edge of the ice cream van counter. I shook my hea

　　　　　i wake next to him so happy, as if it is the sunniest day in history and every yellow wildflower in the world, every primrose, every buttercup, every cowslip, have opened all at once, even though it is the last days of august, and they are all spring flowers—they've all pushed up out of the earth and opened—*just* for me. and for robin remick. for me and for robin remi

     …me and robin remi

     this sounds so good. it's perfection. it's what i've wished for forever, ever since he moved to the village and i met him. two long years of waiting. and now is the begini

{shook my hea}d, encouraged the dark layered ribbons of my hair to close about my face, all apple scented.

'Did he? He didn't say anything? He's a twat,' Jim told me, his little fishes squinting at me.

I shrugged, cast my eyes into the van to receive my sealed-up ice cream-lolly. I just couldn't get myself to agree with Jim Clarke that Robin Remick was a twat. I wished he would leave me alone.

'I'm going over to Rebecca's dad's house to carry on with that job for him after tea,' he said, all sort of gentle. 'I've got the key to the garage. You want to come with? Cycle along with me? He always leaves a stash of biscuits and chocolate bars and sweets there for me.'

I swivelled away, struck out across the green. I ripped the wrapper off of my ice cream, got a hold of its dinky stick, bit through the crisp pink water-ice coat into its creamy vanilla oblong. I drew in a whistling breath of air, fluting the dense melting lump around the inside of my mouth. I examined my teeth-marks in the lolly and the sizable notch I had taken out at its corner, all perfect, like something out of a cartoon. Jim Clarke's footsteps came at me through the ground as he tagged my elbow, his own raspberry Mivvi clutched loosely in his hand, still in the wrapper, like he didn't really want it.

'Come on,' he said.

'Nah,' I told him, licking into my bite-mark.

'It's fun. Why not?'

'Fun to watch you scrape rock-hard bitumen tar stuff, off of a ton

14

of old wood-block flooring with some chisel thing? Huh.'

'Well, not that,' he said. 'I mean, we can loaf about in the garden there. Eat loads of free goodies. No one else is there.'

'You got a key to the house?'

'No. But we can get in a window if you want. I know how because I helped Rebecca get in the other week.'

I sucked off some raspberry shell where a crack had appeared in the bit below the massive crater I had developed. I licked at the vanilla underskirts, which were starting to drip. My teeth hurt all the way back into my mouth where the large chunk of icy creamy cold was rammed. 'That's breaking and entering,' I said all blurry, my tongue slipping around my thawing bounty, saliva building.

'Not really. We're friends. I thought you might like to go back there, that's all.'

'Yes, really,' I slurped. 'It is. And anyway, why would I want to do that? Why would I want to punish myself with memories of beauty turned to pain, huh? Just tell me that?'

'I don't know,' he said. 'Just thought it might help you, that's all.'

'It's going to make me cry more, see.'

'Ah,' he said. And then he indicated with his finger and his fishes, 'You got—er…' and scraped at his own chin with his knuckle. I saw how his fingernails had thick black under them, and that the whorls of his fingertips were stained black too, and my tongue snaked out in the general direction he specified, captured a small slur of milky sweetness. I ignored him as he tried to show me there was more mess on my face, but he kind of arrested me, reached out as if he were going to wipe it off himself, 'You still…' so I quickly dragged the back of my hand over my lips and chin in one foul sweep.

He nodded. 'Yeh, that's it. You got it.'

I didn't tell him I didn't care about ice cream on my chin.

'Look,' he said. 'What I'm saying is, I don't mind. I don't mind if you want to talk about it some mo

itting cross-legged up high on the haystack behind the garage, sun all into my face, wind at my back, i am all kind of warm and cold at the same time, like when you stand in front of a newly lit open fire in a very wintry room. jim clarke is looking at his hands mostly, face set in an expression of pained understanding, occasionally glancing his fishes my wa

i just don't get it, i am saying. how can he just be ignoring me now? i mean, ever since we all got up, he's acted like i don't exist. you know, i went up to him, all smiling, you know, and all thinking something amazing is happening and he just looks right through me and turns away and starts saying something to rebecca in a smiley, even *flirty* kind of a way and... i am sniffing now, dumb, blonde tears ripping down my cheeks, landing on my hands and shining in the sunlight, like they are some kind of ultimate goal, jewels of the soul, gifts i want to give to robin. my throat wracks as my chest caves i

hey, it's alright, says jimbo. he's—i don't know—but if you ask me, he's a tw—

—i'm not asking you what he is. i'm wanting to know what's going on. why would he…i mean, *wh*

i don't know bu—

—well, maybe you could find out, speak to him for me? ask him? could yo

jimbo clarke nods with his whole body. y-yeah… he stutters. yeah, i could do tha

oh god, jimbo, it just felt so good, so nice, i can't believe how it felt and—but oh my *god*, but maybe it's because i—you think it's because i go

16

what? because you got wha

when i pulled away—i got such a shock when he—when he—see? and i pulled back and maybe i offended him? do you think? do you think? ohgod, i was such an idiot, such a—but i didn't mean—so nai

jimbo clarke is staring at me, kind of confused, eyes all slivers of silvery-blue whitebait, his monk hair lighting up like a sort of saint in an old religious painting. and a thought seems to come clear to him, his little fishes suddenly stranded on eyeball beaches; they would be thrashing their tails if they had any—but then i get to see they do—his mind is their tails. i realise he thinks robin remick has tried to do something bad to m

no! i mean, it wasn't anythi—it wasn't *that*. he just—it was just i—arghh—i shouldn't be telling you this, i don't thi

{talk about it some mo}re with me,' Jim Clarke was saying. 'I totally don't mind. I *like* you talking with me. And the shit he's said since—you know, maybe you want to talk about that? Because I *know*—*I know*—he's a lying tosser. I know you didn't do those things. I mean, I *know* you didn't say them or anything.'

'I've talked about it. I talk about it all the time with my friends.'

'Oh.' The weight of that word, the way he let it out, drew me to slide my eye to him. I saw he pressed his lips into themselves, pushed air hard into their closed gate, so the skin around them made small pale balloons. His fishes dragged along the ground.

A drip of my ice cream was making a journey down my wrist to my elbow, red mixed in with the creamy-yellow. I had to lick all around the bottom of the stick, and then i spotted its raspberry jacket was breaking away, about to fall off, so I slurped it up into my mouth, all in one go, saying, 'Mmmmm…' and turned the delicious tangy sweetness around and around with my tongue til it became liquid. It was sort of kissing, I thought. But without all the crazy body response. The thought brought a fizzy tingle between my legs, and I felt myself just a bit disappear. Or reappear more like, like I came wholly into the present, that Consciousness thing my uncle was always going on about—me in this moment, just all Awareness, a part of all everything, connected through this wakened fizz to all the joyous fizz of life.

Jimbo Clarke sighed, but silent. I didn't want to, but he forced me to sense it somehow. 'Okay, well I better get going.'

'Okay.' I absorbed my focus at sucking the rest of my ice cream easily off of the stick as he stood there, sucked at the flat yellowish wood too, so I tasted its nature-flavour too, all mixed in with hints of sugar.

'I'll see you, then,' he muttered.

'Sure.' I glanced up, saw him begin to slope off across the grass. And a sort of stab jerked me into another now, the soft sunlight and the grass swards and the long romantic shadows all crashing in. I swallowed away my pleasure. 'Hey Jimbo,' I called.

He turned. 'Yeh?'

Propelling myself toward him, the sweet sensations recharged, fizzing up my body in a kind of glory; I made my eyes sincere, in a dulling-that-glory kind of a way. I muttered, 'I didn't mean...' I saw his face open. 'I mean, you know, you're my friend too. Of course.'

He made a scrunched sort of smile, half in, half out. 'Ah.'

I shrugged, nose wrinkling. 'It's just girly stuff, see.'

He returned my shrug. 'Is it?'

'Yeah.'

'I see.' One of his pimple-speckled cheeks got kind of sucked into itself. 'Well, I thought we had a good chat that day on the haystack.'

I squawked, all laughy. 'Chat?'

He guffawed, shook his head, reddening. 'Yeh, understatement. You know what I mean.'

'Yeah, I do. Course I do.'

'Anyway…any time…'

I felt a surprising and sudden affection for Jim Clarke right then, and I held his little blue fishes with a closed-lip smile, opening my mouth as if to say something, then just smiling it again.

'See you,' he piped. And 'Hey, you want this?' He offered me his raspberry Mivvi, still in the packet, his tar-blackened crescent moons of fingernails catching the day's late sunlight. I saw his hands were kind of knarly and reddened like he was an old man already.

'Mmm, yeah.'

'It's going to be pretty melty.'

I took it. 'I don't mind; I like it like that. Thanks.'

We split in different directions, me pausing to tear open the bottom of the wrapper super slow, overcome by rampant delight when I managed to extract the melt-sheened ice cream-lolly in one piece, by its stick.

I made my way past the red phone box, through the one-road council estate, and pretended not to look when I passed Tufty's pale-bricked bungalow. I could tell he wasn't looking out for me, so it didn't matter anyway. I reasoned he was probably having his tea or maybe he had gone up to meet Robin at his and was going to have tea there. I felt an even mix of relief and sorriness not to see him. I hoped he wasn't avoiding me. It was obvious he wouldn't want to talk about what had happened—or what hadn't happened, more like—but I liked to think he might still be friendly, even though he was Robin Remick's friend first.

As I approached the sizable tarmacked square at the end of the estate, flanked on two sides by its garages, I heard the bright slap of a football against a garage door, the resulting rattle reverberating through the ribbed pulled-down metal like a distress signal. My hairs went and stood up on some kind of alert. And I was right, because there they were, the two of them, kicking around that ball. When I came into view, just kind of stopped in the wide driveway which opened up to the forecourt, Tufty looked up, all innocent, his white-blonde hair another type of pudding, a longer one, a hangover from the Seventies, silky-as and not remotely tufty or anything. He was younger than us by a couple of years, stark-white, chubby, with the droopy face of a bloodhound.

He raised his hand and I made a pulled-in smile, felt the sticky lolly residue all holding my lips together, tried not to look at Robin, looked at Robin, focused all my efforts on Tufty as I put one foot in front of the other. I felt my body all growing out of itself. But it wasn't nice. It was trembly and heart-ren

eel his leg moving, very gently, under the covers, and then his foot brushes mine and something leaps right in that little bud of me, the most exquisite tugging, rippling in waves from right *there!* *oh!* and up my body, all the way up to my head. everything goes light, weightless, like i might faint, and like maybe bright lights have come on inside my head, and then he does it again and, in all the brilliance, i get to know it wasn't by accident. through all the rippley and wavy, like i'm soft warm toffee, i very slowly move my own foot, aware of keeping the duvet from rustling, lean it against his, and the warmth and the inner poppings *ah!* slowly, slowly we interplay our toes and arches and i feel myself bursting with joyous electric spangles. unbelievable. someone sighs from the heap of bedding on the floor, and we tense, go still, pounding, listening: a boy, he kicks at his sheets, his breath coming in a steady rhythm, for sure a sleeping rhythm; and my boy-robin shifts his body so his shoulder presses into mine. a million volts jolt my insides and i go all quaking, about dying from the ecstasy. after a while he rolls, and his face is somehow in my throat, and all these tiny fluttery kisses, soft as eyelashes, against my yearning skin, they send me into some sort of starkly present oblivio

{trembly and heart-ren}ding and unbearable. Out of the corner of my eye, I saw Robin Remick was just standing there, not looking at me—but I got the impression his energy wanted to look, and I got the sense he felt bad.

'Alright?' I said to Tufty, fake easy in my tone.

'Yeh. How're you doing?'

'Good. Really good.'

Tufty nodded, like the conversation was done.

And I nodded back. Because it was. 'Off home,' I said, indicating with my chin the narrow hentrack at the other end of the garages, the natural short cut I always took. Struck by the stirring beauty of the trail's sultry greens, feeling love all ending, just like the summer, the rip of tears swore at my eyes and I glanced at Robin Remick. He threw his attention to the leather football at his feet, making a show of kicking it about with himself, so I could tell he had been checking me out, even though he tried to pretend he hadn't. I wondered why he had come to play footie right in my pathway home in the first place? I just let myself watch him, his dexterity with the ball, his long bandy legs inside his black school trousers, the way his fingers went all straight with concentration, his crazy unconscious elegance, and how his black hair flopped into his face, like some raven's wing all kissing his eyelids and flapping for kindness from his pale-brown eyes.

My heart opened and skipped and dribbled off, bounced all over the place. I didn't even feel like an idiot when I should have. I thought about the kissing with that other boy this morning and I saw for sure I had been kissing with Robin Remick all along. I saw a sort of likeness in their looks and how the other boy was just nothing to me; I cringed at how this other's darker muddy eyes had had dried yellow sleeps in their corners I had pretended not to see, balked at his crusty smell and unkempt form. I felt a small shard of sorry for him. This boy here, he was proud of his looks, he took good care of himself. I supposed he might have been arrogant. I should have hated myself for loving him, but still I didn't. And then I kind of did a bit. And I kind of hated him too. For ruining everything. For ignoring me the next day, for spreading the rumours about me.

The hurt in my chest burned brightly. School kids believe all these things. Because they want to. And they think they're filthy, shocking. Inside my head, I said to him, You didn't even care enough for our friendship. You betrayed me. And a couple of hot tears flew down my face, fell between my feet, made horrible beautiful dark splashes, all impact and spattered edges, on the tarma

ead bent over the curve of his plastic corner bath, fluffy avocado-green towel all round his shoulders, another protecting his face and his bandaged nose, i direct the flow of water from my friend's fancy gold showerhead. my free hand glides along his neck, guiding the short hairs there into the warm strands of water. his neck is dark browned up to the line of his haircut and i want to kiss it. i would never dare. i'm not sure he feels that way about me. but i am joyful to be touching him so intimately, to be allowed this task of washing his hair, this need he has of me, that it is me he has asked. or maybe i asked him {not sure} {i think—*yes*, i did, i *hinted*} {and then it was *his* idea, see}. the feel of his skin, of his hair, sends a heat hotter than the water up my fingers, flushes up my face, so it burns, and i am glad he can't see me. i get to feel some lovely waves of something in my body, feelings like i get sometimes when i am

22

riding, something that spirals up and down me at once, as if a sunflower is kind of opening in my heart, *oh!* and yes, in *that!* place *oh!* and the sun is shining so bright and moving so fast, and this sunflower is turning its stunning face to follow its rays, turning and turning, in wild spirals in my—*shh!* in french, they call a sunflower a tournesol, turn-with-the-sun, because they do, all day long, until they fold their golden petals back over their faces in the dusky eveni

i realise he has said something when he raises his voi

i say, what? i didn't hear you over the water, se

it's a bit too ho

oh n !

and i reach forward, over the bathtub, my t-shirt catching on the wet edge, feel the delicious tug of it as i adjust the temperature, turning first the co

arrrg !

sorry. and then the ho

arrrg !

sorry. i hold the shower away from his head, testing it with my other hand, and i'm all shaking, starting to laugh and now he's laughing too, turning his head and peering from under his towel so i kind of leap inside of me at his upside-down face in proximity to mine. his teeth have the slightest gaps betwee

silly moo, he tells me, so i hear the lilt of his only-just newcastle accent, his tone all teasing but kind of affectionate to

watch out, i say, dashing my wet hand against his shoulder-towel, all catching the droplets of water running to his bandage. you're getting it we

he blinks water out of his nearest eye, like he's winking. he has kind of dark circles under his eyes, bruising from the operatio

all like he knows i'm thinking about it, he says, d'you

think my nose is going to be better?   when it's healed and the swelling goes dow

> i don't like to tell him i have no idea, so i say, ye
>
> they put a little rod in it, to make up for the broken bridg
>
> i didn't mind it broken anyway, i sa
>
> it was too fa
>
> it was dented. all like a boxer. does it hur

he nods in a sort of determined manner, bringing the dimple back into his smooth brown cheek, eyes crinkling. it's going to be better. for sure, defin

{on the tarma}c, all like it had rained just two drops out of the blue. I kicked across the dumb tears with the toe of my black school shoe, killing them. Just like Robin Remick had killed our friendship. Tufty yelled out something to him, bulldozed toward him, going for the ball, stampeded after him as Robin dribbled it away. I smiled. I would normally have laughed and yelled and joined in. I wafted across the black square of man-keeping-nature-out, noting how man couldn't really manage this for long—there were cracks all over the place, eruptions, fantastic wounds, with all kinds of grass stems and pretty weedy flowers growing out of them. Red poppies bobbed their delicate heads along the wall-line between the garage doors. I took myself into that line, paused at the last corner of yellow brick garage to reach for a white bindweed flowerhead, pinched my forefinger and thumb around the soft green swelling at its base, the sound of the boys playing together scorching me like freezing cold water racing down my spine. I prepared, all saying inside my head, Gran-nyyyy...*POP out of bed!* exerted pressure, so the silky trumpet popped right out of its little green bed, which was really its sepal, and was more like a fairy cup. Ejected upward, the flower made an arc before smashing to my feet.

I threw open the back door to our white stucco house, gravel echoing like harsh laughter, my body in a sheen of sweat, breath all tearing from running like crazy with my canvas school bag jolting against my ribs—*this little piggy cried wee-wee-wee! all the way home!* My boxer dog rushed at me, all barking, squealing, smiling, nails ticking and clicking on the kitchen tiles.

'Birdie, Birdie!' I cast off my bag, heard its satisfying smack to the floor, slapped at the dog's honey-coloured flanks so she yelped her pleasure.

'Hello, lovey,' called my mum through the din, looming toward us from the dining room. 'How was your day?'

'Birdie-girl!' Tail whipping against my calves, the dog careened around me. 'Good girl. Good girl.'

'Lovey—*lovey*—'

'Here, Birdie-girl.' I threw my hand up, directing her to jump up at it, and she snapped at the air, took to howling. I bent to her, howled back in her face, felt her breath steamy and stinky.

'Sweetheart. Will you *stop* it? You're totally winding her up.'

Springing right up, hands like claws, I barked into my mum's face, and my dog copied me, pitched herself at her. My mother started shouting a whole lot of drama at us, all stuff about how Birdie was too old for this and it was bad for her heart, and I was too old for it too and what was I playing at, all this coming through our barks until, pretty soon, we both got the message, kind of stopped at the same time and we all three stood there dumbly.

To the dog, my mum said, 'Now go and *sit*.' And she pointed into the open dining room door. 'Go to your chair. *Now*. Go on.' Birdie put her bum down where she was, went all guilty looking, her curved bony tail slapping against the floor, the white tip of it waving always upward. 'For god's sake, Birdie. Will you *listen*?'

25

'Hey Birdie.' I stroked my fingers through the white flame of her furrowed forehead, bent as I picked up her sloppy jowls in the cup of my hand. 'Go on, now.' I stoppered my tongue at the entrance of my mouth, made kissy noises into hers. Her long pink flesh lolloped out, all like a serpent, slurped across my chops so fast and I laughed and said, 'Errrr', as I wiped her slobber into the crook of my sleeve.

My mum tutted, blew an over-the-top sigh. 'How many—oh, what's the point? If you get worms, it will be your own doing.'

'There's a good girl,' I told Birdie, patting her. 'Go on, now. Do as you're told.' The dog clicked off and I watched her cross the dining room, hop up heavy-as, into her Egyptian-blue threadbare armchair. She curled, settled her head on extended paws, eyes regarding me, all serious.

'Now…' said my mother. 'What's going on?'

'Nothing.'

'I *know* you. What's up? Are you alright?'

I shrugged. 'Yeh, course I am.'

'You look like you've been crying.'

'What, me?'

'Well, who else?'

I peeled my lower lip down into my chin, feeling the air on my exposed inner flesh, eyes widened. My mother stared at me and when I released my face, she puffed a smile through her nose, shook her dark head. I could see she'd just had her hair done, freshly blacked and blow-dried, all tipped under and superhero-shinied.

'Hair looks nice.'

She sort of glowed straight away. 'You noticed.'

'I always notice. I'm starving. Have we got any crisps?'

'No, love. Tomorrow.'

'*Fry*—' I said in slow motion '—*day*. Duh…'

26

'Yes…' She made her dark blue eyes round-as, nodded in mock response, then said, all kind of proud and like she was responsible for my wit, 'Clever clogs.' I pretended I was opening a packet of crisps and exaggerated putting a really big one in my gob, making crunching noises. 'Maybe have a slice of toast, love.'

'With jam, can I?'

'No. Have peanut butter.'

I shook my head, half-closed my eyes. 'But-er…'

'Butter's fine, of course.'

'But—er—what if I want…ham?'

She held up her finger. '*One* slice.'

'Got'cha.'

'Dinner will be ready at six-thirty—when your father gets home.'

I became aware of the smell of something delicious and the whirr and heat of the oven. 'Shepherd's pie?' She smiled, assented, awarding me that same self-satisfied look. 'Isn't he cycling tonight?'

'No, there's a documentary on BBC2 he wants to watch.'

'Wow,' I stated, flat-as. 'Dad is a rebel, huh? Against himself? You think that's where I get it?'

She chuckled. 'I don't know about that. Perhaps you get it from me. I'm sure he'll make up for it at the weekend and we won't see him all Sunday.'

'You? You must be joking.' I started for the door.

'Aren't you having your toast, love?'

'Can't be bothered. Why doesn't he just video tape it?'

'I don't know—ask him. I thought you were starving?'

'Only people in very poor countries are starving, Mrs.'

'Yes.'

'And also maybe some of the ones from your work maybe.'

'Yes. Sometimes they are.' She cleared her throat. 'If they come in

27

off the streets. Certainly, they are malnourished. But quite right, we shouldn't be saying "starving", should we?'

I grinned. 'I *did* say it first.'

'You did.'

'And you *didn't* tell me off.' I flicked my bottom up at her, like a donkey bucking at the beach, made a braying sound, and darted off through the dining room, intent on the living room and the TV, which I could hear was already on.

'Bag, lovey.'

I huffed as I went back, swinging out my leg as a lever to balance myself, swept up my canvas satchel by its snaky strap, said, 'You calling me an ol' bag?' and narrowed my eyes, sucked in my cheeks, staggered off all leaning on an imagined stick. Her laughter chimed after me.

Entering the living room, I found my sister slobbed out across the olive-green velour settee with her snub-nosed frizzy-haired friend.

'I didn't know you were here,' I said to the friend.

'Well, you do now,' quipped my sister. 'Mastermind.' And they both tittered.

'How comes you weren't on the bus?'

'Mr Griggs drove us.'

'Mr Grimms,' said her friend. And they tittered some more.

'How come?'

My sister took out a small white paper bag from where she had it nestled against her thigh, fiddled her fingers inside it, eyes feasting. She went for a Fried Egg, bit into its dense chewy sweetness as she offered the open bag for her friend to eyeball. Frizz-head chose a miniature Cola bottle, stretched its neck between her teeth until it snapped, made a lip-smacking sound, all grinning at me daft-as. My sister held out the bag to me so I had no choice but to go over and decide on a sweet.

'Can I have two?' I asked.

'No.'

'Oh, go on—I'm going up to my room.'

'Okay then. But leave me a couple of Flying Saucers. A pink one. And the yellow one.'

I fished out a pink Flying Saucer, showed her with a fake toothy grin, said, 'There's another,' stuffed it in my mouth.

'I know, you twerp.'

I let the flavourless pink rice-paper dissolve on my tongue, relished the release of the fizzing sherbet, didn't say mmmm, though I wanted to, picked out a Rhubarb-and-Custard, and held it out for them to see. 'Let me have a Black Jack too?'

'No more. Get your own if you want more.'

'O-*kay*.' I chucked the sweet bag at her friend, started out the room.

'And say thank you.'

'Thanks, sis.'

'And don't call me sis.'

'Okay, sis-*duh*.'

Her friend giggled. 'Hey, wait.' She took out another Cola bottle, made sure she had my attention as she kissed her lips right over it, freed it, held it out to me all shiny with her spit. 'Want it?'

'No, I do not.' I slid my eyes to my sister, 'Duh,' exactly as she spawned some "excellent" idea and sprung herself like the granny flower, in an arc, for the crunkled white paper bag. I turned my back in disgust.

'Wait! Wait, wait!'

I passed through the doorway into the dining room, while she yelled my name. Under my breath, I said, 'Naff off.'

She was laughing and shouting, bashing the sofa forcefully, 'Here girl. Good doggie. Come on, girl,' and shrieking on about how she'd give me more sweets and, 'Come on now, girl.'

I swung past Birdie, who was wagging her tail, levering herself out of her chair. 'Hey baby, they don't mean you.' I patted my hip. 'Come on, come upstairs with me.'

My dog gave me a tired kind of a look, trotted off to the calling, tail all up and full of energy. A huge heave in my chest, I slipped around the table, which stood at the bottom of the doored-off staircase, thumbed open the latch, was about to take the stairs, when out popped my mum.

'What's going on, girls?' She caught sight of me. 'Sweetheart? What…'

I swung back, held her eye, made a one-shouldered shrug, flicked my eyes up to heaven and back. 'Nothing. They're just idiots.'

'Girls?'

I heard my sister and her friend stop momentarily, like a kind of gasp, then peel into wind-up laughter. 'Don't bother,' I said to my mum. 'They're not worth it.'

She gave me one of her impressed looks. 'Best to just ignore them, huh?'

I saw she held a cup of tea and a blue-flowered side-plate with a pink tongue of ham on a slice of toast. 'That for me?'

She stepped toward me, offering them up. 'Who else?'

I smiled. 'You made it for me.'

'Yes. I'm a sucker, you think?'

I took the little plate. 'Why, thank you kindly,' I warbled, in my best Southern-belle voice. '"I have always depended on the kindness of strangers."'

She chuckled. 'Blanche Dubois? *Streetcar Named Desire*. Very good.'

We held a prolonged moment, then I turned and sprung up the stairs. I got to wonder what I might become when I grew up, found myself singing, '*Only the crumbliest, flakiest chocolate, tastes like chocolate never tasted before…*'

Scrabbling in my bag, I tossed some books and folders onto the flowery duvet cover, selected my English homework, settled myself with my back up the wall. I tried to read my notes from class for the essay I had to write. I crunched through my wholemeal toast with its sweet salty ham. I tried not to think of Robin Remick. But I saw him, just about like he was in the room, and he was grinning at me with his gappy teeth, face all flushed up. All kinds of butterflies came fluttering out of his mouth, whispering their wings against my throat. I slumped, wriggled myself down into the bed, let the half-eaten toast lay beside me on its plate, feet kicking my schoolwork away into a commotion of hard thumps and sshy papers.

And pretty soon, I was floating, all kind of easy, naked toes teased by his, little jolts spiralling from my own sweet—I saw I had a wild pink rosebud tucked between my legs—it was opening, like lips in a pouty kiss—and my whole body was opening up, into a cerulean blue sky, arms ecstatic branches reaching, reaching—body a river, bright ripples of joy—

—ripped back by a succession of rapid raps at my door. The world crashed in as a harsh hurting blur, my heart fast and poundy and high in my ears, eyes blinking hard together and splaying apart as I tried to find focus. I realised my sister was calling my name, all clenched teeth, kind of keeping it quiet, at the same time delivering a whole lot of velocity.

Cells vibrating all out of sync, my voice came thickened, hoarse. 'What? What do you want? Just come in if you have to.'

'It's locked,' she hissed, showing me by rattling the doorknob, weight bumping the glossy white wood. 'What are you up to?'

'Nothing.'

'Are you going to let me in or what?'

I rolled onto my side to face her voice. 'Or what.'

'Huh? *What*?'

'Equals, "no".'

She gave out an exasperated sigh but didn't walk off. Her feet shifted. Her voice went whispery. 'I *really* think you should let me in. There are things…'

And then I got it. 'Ah. Hang on.' I levered myself to sitting, swung my feet in their white ankle socks to the pale-green carpet. I felt my whole inside-body all wobbly, kind of sprawling, as I flicked back the little brass lock.

'You've got *major* control issues,' she said, pushing past me into room.

'Yeh. Right.'

She plonked herself onto my bed, stared at me pretty severely, like she was waiting for me issue forth some sort of confession.

'Where's your friend, then?' I said.

'My *friend*. Has gone *home*. For her *dinner*.'

'She's not staying here to eat then?'

'She's *gone*. Dummy. Were you asleep? You were, weren't you?'

'So?'

'You literally have no idea, do you?'

'I actually do.'

'I heard these terrible rumours about you today.'

'What rumours?'

'I thought you said you—like you don't know what I'm talking about.'

'I might not know. There's all kinds of rumours. But some are old news now, see.'

She stared at me for a long moment. 'Okay then.'

My tongue went and fiddled about with a strand of ham I hadn't realised was stuck in between a couple of lower molars. And with this, appeared a kind of stoppered sideways smile.

'Do you think this is funny? I mean, I'm literally freaking out right now—and you're—'

'—what do *you* think?'

'Well, I don't think it's funny, for a start. You *do* know what people are saying?'

I nodded, kept nodding, all biting my lower lip, soaking up the pause. 'It's the way you say "literally".'

'For god's sake, girl. People are talking about you and saying that you—that you might have—they're saying you're...*showing off* actually, that you've *DONE it*—with that Robin Remick boy. And a load of other disgusting stuff too.'

'Oh—so you believe I'm telling everyone I fucked Robin Remick? And you believe I did it too? Do you? Because I'm not quite sure who's the mad one around here.'

'I don't know, I-I—' I saw how her cheeks flared up, her eyes leaving mine, darting about the carpet '—I wish you wouldn't use that awful word.'

'Well, that's what the rumours say, isn't it? They don't say "Done it".'

Her voice came out in a rasp. 'No. No, they don't.'

'No. Because rumours are harsh. And made up and meant to hurt and cause some kind of trouble, see. For god knows why.'

'So it wasn't you who said it?'

'Duh...I didn't say it and I didn't do it.'

She kind of sagged, hand coming up to her heart, eyes rolling back. 'Oh, thank god…thank god…'

I stared at her. 'What exactly do you think of me?'

And then she bolted upright, eyeballing me all hard. 'But did you do *anything* with him? This is all coming out of—because of you staying over at Rebecca Hogarth's last Saturday, isn't it?'

'It is "coming out of" that, yeah.'

'So why on earth would this get started? Did you do *anything*?'

I shrugged. 'We slept in the same bed.'

'You did *what*?'

'Nothing.'

'Are you *mental*? You—you sle—Mum would kill you—'

'—oh, so you're going to run and tell our mum now? I knew I shouldn't have said anything. I mean, why would I trust *you*? Really?'

'No, no, I'm not. Of course not—you can trust me—I want you to trust me—but—did you let him-let him…? I mean, is it true, the other…?'

My sights went and flitted around the floor. 'We didn't do anything. I am totally innocent.'

'Oh god, so it's true, he…he-he—arrgh!—he *fingered* you, did he?—I *hate* that I have to say that word.'

'No. I didn't even know what fingered meant until all this started.'

'And now you do?'

'Well, yes. I had to find out, didn't I? I had to find out what I was supposed to have done. Everyone seems to think it's the ultimate, most disgusting thing. But surely, it's just touching and it's natural, anyway?'

'No. Where do you get that idea?'

'It's just another part of the body. I've felt myself *there* for years, all when I'm riding and stuff. It's nice. I just don't get why it's so bad.'

She made an abrasive kind of breath deep in her chest. 'Can you *one hundred* percent guarantee you didn't let him?'

'He didn't even try.'

'He didn't? Are you sure?'

'I think I would know.'

'And you better not be saying all that stuff about it being nice and natural to anyone. They're going to think *you're* disgusting—and dirty, that's what—they're going to think you *did* do it and they'll think you're a slag.'

I shrugged, looked down at my thumbnail pressing into my forefinger so the flesh went kind of white around it. 'You do know how old I am?'

'Did you already say it? To who? And I *do* know how old you are and you're way too young to be doing any of this, or even talking about it.'

'To *whom*,' I said. 'Rebecca and Debbie, that's all. It's fine, they're my friends.'

'And what did they say?'

I made a kind of sighing sound. 'Exactly that. They think it's disgusting and something they would never do.'

'And they're right.' Her mouth went into a tight little line. 'But who started thi-this rubbish? That's what I want to know. Do you know? Because I'll—I tell you, I'll—' she shook her head, eyes all sharp like knives were bursting out of them.

A smile puffed out of me, and I felt all like some kind of red-faced robin flew free from my chest. 'Because you'll what?'

'I don't know—but *no one* makes up stuff like that about my little sister and gets away with it. I'll hit someone if I have to.' I gazed at her in a kind of dazed wonder. And suddenly I felt all this hot and slimy stuff gathering up inside of me. I worked hard not to let it out.

The thought dropped how I never wanted Robin Remick to fly free from my chest. I wanted him caged there forever.

'Hey,' she said. 'Hey, it's alright. She rose and rubbed at my shoulder. I realised I was sniffling. 'Come on, we'll get the truth out there—I mean, not about the *bed*—' she made a kind of smirk which came with a curbed, scratchy laugh in her throat '—you idiot—we'll get the truth out that it's all lies. It will be alright; it really will. I promise. What is it Uncle Gordie is always saying? It will all pass?'

I nodded. 'This too shall pass.'

'Yes, that's it: this too shall pass.' She nodded, all going somewhere into herself, growing a frown. 'Hey, you think it was one of the others who stayed at Rebecca's, that spread this horrible rubbish? Where did everyone else sleep? Didn't you say there was eight of you? Hey, and you never said what you *did* do? Huh? You've got to tell me. Did you snog? Or wha

nd all these tiny fluttery kisses, soft as eyelashes, against my yearning throat, they send me into some sort of starkly present oblivion, like all of life is condensed and kind of painful and ecstatic at once and like i am the whole of the night sky outside of the roof, all its stars, the moon, the planets; i am the sun on the other side of the world, shining all over australia. and yet i am me, me and robin remick, we both, in this bed, i am the biggest, most blessed and beautiful me possible, spilling my edges. i have surely melted into him. *oh robin!* i trill inside of my own skull. robin. i love you. his face moves to mine, his lips touching mine, explosions erupt and magnify, and i will surely die, perhaps i *am* dying. i am crazy for him, craz—but then—*eergh!* the recoiling, me turned solid, snapping, a red elastic band breaki—*eergh!* what?—his tongue—thick and hot and wet—*oh eegh!* i didn't expe—i didn't expect—it comes out of the oblivion, and it scares the joy out of me, just for a second, enough that he

36

disappea

{Or wha}t?' she was saying, all tender.

My head was just shaking on its own, all kind of hanging down, my lips pressed together. How could I have been such an idiot? I am sorry, so sorry, because I see I drove him away. And kissing with your tongue is natural and fantastic. When I let my lips go, I said, 'We did nothing. Just nothing. Our feet just touched—footsies, it was—that's all.'

Hypericum Fireworks

Stepping out from the shade of the covered entranceway, the stark sunshine just about blinded me, and everyone went all nuclear explosion. I tried not to stumble as I took myself at a snail's pace down the main steps, threading my way between the chattering twos and threes and groups of kids—all ages from eleven, which were the newbie first-year rabble, up to fifth-formers mostly—as well as a single cluster of sixth-form boys who looked totally like men, but still kind of stupid and wide-eyed, for sure prone to head-butting each other like some kind of boy-giraffe from a David Attenborough wildlife programme. I felt a couple of those last staring at me, felt the burn of their gaze into my bum at it moved under the pleats of my grey school skirt, pretended not to hear when one made a witless low whistle, called out my name. I knew which one it was: he had beachy hair, pale skin, bulbous red lips, blue eyes; he was Danish, still had the remnants of an accent, and his body was kind of magazine-perfect, the muscles in his arms, his strapping height and narrow hips, the thrill of too many a girl. I dipped down onto the forecourt, pretended not to look in the direction of the bike sheds as I scanned across the vista of the low-slung Seventies school buildings. Just for a change, I got hypnotized by the masses of yellow hypericum flowers adorning the shrubs in the narrow earth-beds along the retaining walls, felt myself pulled by their insistent faces, was forced to make a detour, went and picked one. I jammed it into my nose, its firework stamens causing the anticipated whizzy delight of a starburst sneeze— all glitter and wink rousing those parts of my body I now knew I wasn't supposed to know about. Taking a side-eye shufti, I saw old white-head still watching and I couldn't decide if I liked it or hated him—but I savoured the sense of my own internal fireworks, felt a Catherine wheel wheeling around and around, making high-pitched shrieks with sparks spraying everywhere as I walked. I stuck the flower into the link of my golden chain from which my Snoopy pendant hung, so all you might see were his darling little running feet.

The bike sheds were not yet visible, stood a ways off to the right. You had to go up round the back a bit to get to them. I flared my vision to take in the whole landscape—the school car park, the road and hedgerows, the lusty trees and yellow stubble wheat fields, beyond which there were hints of the village. My attention was focused to check whether my new friend was in view. I wanted to get to our meeting point after her; did not want to be hanging around the bike sheds first, and was intentionally nearly ten minutes late, more now, I supposed, since I had dawdled. Not finding her anywhere, I figured she must be there—and waiting for me. My goal was out of bounds during the day, and not somewhere I had any reason to frequent at any time, so in case I had the eyes of any teachers, I made it look like I was headed to the road leading to the train station. I was ready to pretend I was going into town over lunchtime to meet my mum—for what, I hadn't decided. The dentist maybe. Or the doctor. Or maybe we had to buy me an outfit for a wedding we were going to and for some reason this was the only possible window. I actually found myself starting along that road, caught by my own spin, made a decision—bugger it—I was going to town. I would call my mum, tell her I wasn't feeling so good, meet up with her at her work. I would miss the afternoon lessons of history and maths, my least favoured subjects, and she would write me a note for the next day.

'Oi,' I heard. 'Oi, you.' It was a male voice, quite deep, and I felt a shudder scud over my shoulders. Footsteps were raining fast behind me. I sped up, kept right on going, like I was full of rights. I started singing quite loudly, as a cover for my contrived ignorance. But finally, my name was yelled. And I turned, still singing, all full of confidence, because I knew who it was. 'Where are you off to?' he asked, beachy hair all blazing up in the sun.

I shrugged. 'What's it to you?'

'You're out of bounds, for starters.'

'So?'

He grinned, eyes all kind of eating me up. 'You're really bad at singing—you know that? Seriously out of tune.'

I wrinkled my nose, frowned, like there was a dodgy smell coming off of him.

'So where are you going?' His voice went soft and he jutted out his chin, made it all dimply, fat lips pressed together in a smile.

'Nowhere.'

He nodded. 'Ah…'

'Nowhere—with *you*.'

He laughed. 'You've got some balls.'

'No. No, I haven't. I'm a female.'

His whole body fired up laughing, and he stepped toward me and I felt like he was going to get a hold of me. I was treading backward, him all growing on me, and there came the slip of the gravel on the road beneath my clunky school shoe and I was sort of losing my foothold, all kind of reeling backward—and the trees were flying downward, the sky moving higher, all blue filling my field of vision and—he grabbed a hold of my arm, yanked me upright, yelling out, 'Watch it!' and pulling me into him. My body went into some kind of auto-kick mode, feet cracking into his shins, wrenching itself out of his grip.

'Get off me. Get off.'

His hands flew up on either side of his head—and I saw a cowboy in a movie, all like I held a gun on him. 'Hey, easy, easy.' And a stream of words in what I presumed was Danish; a flash of passion in his eyes. And a grin and I think he called me tiger and seemed to be coming to grab me again.

'Copenhagen,' came a shrill cry.

We both turned to see my Prefect sliding into view.

'Hey,' I said, as greeting, wiping the back of my hand under my nose, all kind of sniffing with attitude.

'Turner,' he said. 'What gives? You racist cow.'

'Get off my turf.'

'Your turf?'

She pulled up alongside us, nodded her dark head slowly, eyes slapping up at him from way below his massive frame. 'Ye-ah.'

'That's a new one,' he said.

'Hardly.' She skimmed her look to me, indicated toward the school, with her chin. 'I've got this. Go on.' But I just stood there.

'God only knows how you got to be a Prefect,' he said.

'And everyone else knows why you didn't.'

41

He said something in Danish again. It was obvious he was swearing.

'Yeh. Exactly,' she said. 'You prove my point.'

He smiled. 'You know you look quite edible when you're angry.'

'O-kay,' she said. 'Good to know.' She eyeballed him for quite a few beats, made an exaggerated frown. 'What exactly were you up to just now?'

'What exactly are *you* up to?'

She turned her eye to me. 'What are *you* up to? Out here?' The insistence in her look told me to play along. 'Are you planning on skipping class?'

I fidgeted with my feet, looked down. 'Um...no...I was just taking a walk, see.'

'A walk? You can do that around the playing field. You are not allowed to leave the school premises in school hours. I really ought to report you.'

He cut in, saying, to me, 'So you want to go out sometime? I'll take you to the Corn Exchange on Saturday night, how about it?'

'No thanks.'

'A bunch of us go every Saturday—you just let me know when you want to come.'

'Sure thing,' the sixth-form girl said. 'Much obliged.' She raised her finger to me. 'Just this once, I'm going to let you off—because of this lug.'

'Your *turf*,' he said, hissing out a laugh. And to me, 'She's one tough cookie, eh? Watch out for this one.'

As he veered off, I became aware her eyes were fixed on me, and I met them, puffed a smile. 'You always seem to be in boy-trouble, huh?' she said.

I bent, retrieved my firework flower from where it had fallen on the tarmac. I held it out to her. 'For you.'

She took it, placed it behind her ear. 'Come on, you.' She grasped a hold of my hand a moment, let it go, started back the way she had come, and the two of us made a soft leap over the ditch at the edge of the field she had cut across, plunged into the long dry grass. Once we were a way in, she said, 'Here will do nicely,' dropped herself to sitting, crossing her feet on stretched-out legs. I sat beside her. 'Where were you off to? You *do* know the bike sheds are *that* way.' Her thumb jutted out past her yellow flower, pointing behind us.

My lips twisted to one side. 'Yeh.'

'You want to go into town? In a bit?'

I nodded. I felt like she had read my mind. 'Yeh.'

She mirrored my nod. 'I have a free period.'

'Hmmm.'

'You will be skiving…'

I chuckled. She was taking out a packet of fags from her denim jacket pocket.

She wore the same grey cords as the other day. I wished I didn't have to wear school uniform. 'Where did you get those super-tight trousers?' I asked. 'I've never seen them so tight.'

'I took them in myself.' She flipped the lid of her cigarettes, offered me the open pack. 'Want one?'

'Nah.'

'You don't smoke?'

I shrugged, pulled my mouth down. 'Don't feel like it.'

'You don't smoke.'

My head sort of jerked as I smiled. I took the box from her, ran my fingers over the tops of the filters. I wanted to liken them to a brigade of soldiers. I sniffed them. I thought I was going to take one, show her I smoked, but I furrowed up my whole face, it felt, said, 'They

43

smell…*hideous*.'

She grabbed back the box, inhaled it, made an expression all like she was supping at a rose. 'Mmmm…' I watched as she struck a match, lit the frazzled dark-gold end of one, pulled on it, so it went all red and fire and the paper sucked away into the air and I could hear a faint fizzing sound. She drew the smoke into her lungs. I saw the thickness of it pause and lick at the entrance of her mouth, disappear into her. The cigarette made a beautiful delicate grey lace at its end. As she threw back her head, puffing out a stream of haze, the ash fell away into the spray-on grey of her legs, all camouflaged, so only I would ever know it was there.

I chucked myself backwards into the turf, the tasselled yellowed grasses prickling me, making me really awake, all kind of nice in some funny way. 'Ahhhhh,' just came out of me. She let herself slump beside me. I gazed up at the picture-book sky. She chugged on her stinky fag, blew the smoke up with a whole lot of force so I saw it fan out, then dissipate to nothing. 'I didn't know about this place,' I said.

'It's out of bounds.'

'It's nice.'

'Yeah…'

'*This* is kind of nice, huh?'

She made a little noise of assent. And we just stayed like that, quiet, for quite a while, both skydiving, just her one arm moving the cigarette to and from her mouth, and her exaggerated puffing-out breaths. When her cigarette was finished, she half-sat up, stubbed it out on the ground on the other side of her, twisted to lie on her side, all leaning her face into the hand of her crooked elbow, so she could view me. Her other hand fished in her back pocket, produced a tube of Polos, her thumb finding the slice of space between the first two, pushing the top one out and straight into her mouth.

'You're a third-year, aren't you?'

I shrugged, eyes dulled.

She put the packet back in her pocket, hips wriggling slightly. 'You don't look it—but you know that, don't you?'

'Not really…'

'I've been doing my investigations,' she murmured, one eyebrow raising. She moved the Polo against her teeth, so it clicked about.

'Oh?'

'Yup.'

As she slurped on the mint, I started to wonder if she was going to ask me about the rumours and I felt the heat rise in my cheeks. 'Isn't it a bit weird, you making friends with a third-former, then?'

She stared at me for what felt like too long, her eyes all kind of hooded. 'Hmm…could be.'

'So why…?'

'You're not like everyone else, I suppose. Alice. So what's happening with your boyfriend?'

'He's not my boyfriend.'

'He's not your boyfriend?'

I giggled. 'No. Definitely not.'

'He was quite an idiot.'

'Yeah…'

'You were too, to let him kiss you—if you ask me.'

'Oh.'

'So what else did you do with him?'

'But I'm *not* asking you though, am I?'

'Did you let him touch you…?' She made a Leonardo Da Vinci pointing finger, reached over me, landed it right on the crack of skin at my waist. '…here?' I guffawed. Her finger was warm; it felt sweet,

45

like a sweet, like a sherberty sweetie. She lifted her digit about an inch above my body, traced its profile, playing at being a sloth until she reached my boob. Her hand splayed, all like she was about to grasp it, floated just above my grey jersey. 'Here?' I bit my lip, nodded, eyes now fixed to her dark shining globes. I felt a sort of pull and my body made a tiny jerk. 'Yes,' she said, like she meant about the ripple of sequins sparkling within me. She drove her hand at great speed through the air above me and my head lifted to follow, and she hovered it over my skirt, right at the dip in the fabric where my thighs met, pointed downwards, made a pretty arc of her finger. 'How about here?'

I felt myself go all wavy. 'No.'

'But you would have let him if I hadn't come in...'

'No.'

'No? You sure?'

My breath was coming ragged. Concentric circles seemed to emanate from where her finger floated, radiate through my whole being, like I was water and she had penetrated my surface.

'You have very unusual eyes,' she told me, kind of hoarse. 'You know that? Like a soft wintery sky.' She held the Polo between her front teeth, stuck the tip of her tongue into the hole, looped the sweet back into her dark. 'Want one?'

'Yeh...'

She showed it to me again. 'This one?'

The flush that came through me had electricity in it. I might have made a sort of smile, but frowning too, and I heard the rush of my own breath and her breath with her velvet voice in it and the swish and swirl of the grasses under her knees and the hiss of her jacket as her hands came either side of my head and she dipped her face down into mine, hair falling in quiet waves so it kissed her cheeks, and mine too. She looked like a glamorous pop star, mouth all pouting, sticky-looking and like she wore lipgloss all of a sudden. She dipped nearer, paused to stare at me close-up, so she went blurred and I could smell the mint, behind it the stench of the cigarette, and just like that, the Polo was in my mouth with her tongue, and her lips were all pressing into mine, sucking on my lips and my tongue and the Polo on my tongue, and I was sucking on her and the mint and a whole lot of spit.

I couldn't believe I was being kissed by a girl. A sixth-former girl. And I was kissing her back. I didn't even know girls kissed. And her hand really was on my boob and she climbed on top of me, spreading her legs over my pelvis, pressing hers into mine, all the time keeping with the kissing and my body was all kind of mush, like I was dissolving, but it was moving too and pushing itself into her and I was lava again, spurting red hot orange yellow black grime grind I was boundless so hot my voice making gasps and Oooos and all kinds of singing with hers. Her fingers were somehow digging into me, over my skirt, going under my skirt and I—

'—oh my god—stop—oh fu—oh—'

—was struggling to get out from under her and she was shoving herself off of me, all saying something, I didn't know wha

       unning fast across the junior school playing field, i am all laughter and delight, crazy fear all rushing in my chest too, the thump of the boy's seven-year-old feet echoing mine, mad screeches screaming out of me—not feeling his footfalls and turning my head, seeing he is lagging, as he always does, behind. i slow, and slow some more, and he's on me, taking hold of my shoulders in his hands, from behind, yelling, got ya! i pass my eyes over his delicious face, sag my body, moan out, oooo, as he says, c'mon, and holds me by the arm all the way back to base, to the white goalpost, where the other kids are gathered, all the girls caught easily, way before me. he pulls me onto the grass with him, manoeuvres me onto my back and i let him, i always do, don't know why, and he lies on top of me, presses right into me and starts kissing me, meeting my lips with his little ones hard. and he does what he does, starts grinding his hips into mine, back and forth, all still keeping his tight budded mouth on mine, whilst me, i'm saying, fuck, fuck, fucking hell. and i don't know why i'm saying it or what he's doing, but i *do* know, and i start to get upset, and i'm all kicking at him, pushing him off, pulling myself up. i am burning with heat. tears spring, but i hold them back saying, that's it! i'm not playing any mo

{didn't know wha}t she was saying to me, or what had just happened, or what I was doing, or what I wanted—or anything. I scurried a few paces on my shins, scraping my skin on the rough spikey grasses, right through my socks, and sort of nestled up into myself, legs drawn up, my face all in my hands. And I realised I was crying, quite full-on.

'Hey,' she said. 'Hey, it's alright…I wouldn't…I won't…I thought you wanted to.'

All snuffly, I said, 'I don't know…I maybe don't know anything anymore…'

She raised herself up on high knees, made to shuffle towards me, stopped herself. 'You want—can I put my arm around you? I'm really sorry, I didn't mean to upset you. I thought you liked it.'

'I did…' I wailed. 'It's just…'

Her arm curled around my shoulder and she pulled my face into her chest, all kind of kind and like a mother. She let me cry out a whole lot of mess into her denim jacket, so afterwards there were distinct shapes of my wet eyes and sheeny snot and saliva left there, all like a mask of me in negative. When she looked down and saw it, she wiped at it with a sort of affection. She said something about how she forgot how young I was and I told her I really wasn't that young and she said she was really bad at containing herself, she should have waited, she was always getting into trouble, and we just lay back down in the grass together, me on her damp shoulder, all up against her, our arms about each other. I told her all about Robin Remick, right down to how I felt about him, discovered she hadn't heard the rumours, and we rabbited on to each other quite a bit about our families, her forever arguing mum and dad, my older sister, her little brother, my uncle too, in Ireland now, his racehorses, and me helping with training them and how I had wanted to be a jockey but had gotten way too tall. The sun shone down on us, mellow and soothing-as, and after a while we fell asleep, all easy and together in breath and being…

I woke to the feel of her stirring, became cognisant the bell was ringing from way off, gentle, like a bit of foreign birdsong when normally it jarred right through you. We pulled ourselves out of our embrace and up into sitting, we both. She twisted her wrist to look at her watch.

'End of third period. Do you want to go back to class or…?'

'Or,' I stated.

The smile she flashed showed happiness and I knew I reflected the same, felt instantly kind of shy and took to adjusting my knee-high socks, straitening the twists and pulling out the bits of grass seed snagged in them, tugging the elastic against the edge of my knees.

'Don't be snapping your elastic,' she said, one eyebrow raising.

Lewd, I thought, all Shakespearean inside of myself in that sweet moment. I decided not to say it, though. I thought about saying, instead, Why not? in that same kind of way, wished I could raise one eyebrow and all, but swallowed the impulse down, knowing it might rouse her—and even me maybe too.

'We have to lay low for about ten minutes, til everyone's involved in lessons. So no one will see us. I know a back way to the station.'

'You've done this before?'

'Ye-ah. All. The. Time.'

'So how come you *are* a Prefect? That Copenhagen prat has a point.'

'Cheek. I'm a natural leader. Hey, have you got anything to eat? I'm starving.'

Scratchy Yellowed Grasses

We were on the move from one class to another, navigating the streams of kids flowing every-which-way right where the corridors made a kind of crossroads, all hugging our English and Geography folders, elbows jutted, doing our damnedest not to get mashed.

'God, what do you think?' Rebecca was screeching over the din. 'You think he looked at me? Do you? Do you?'

'I think he did, Becca,' said Debbie, tossing the permed curls of her short-back-and-sides blondie locks. 'I'm pretty sure, yes.'

Rebecca all eyeballed me, so I said, 'I'm not sure. I didn't see him do it, but he kind of looked like he just had, right when I looked at him. I think.'

'Yeah,' chimed Debbie, blue eyes spangling.

'Oh my god!' Rebecca sounded like she had a stick up her bum. 'I like him soooooo much.'

'You don't say,' I said.

She jabbed me in the ribs, 'Oi!' She was stoppering her laugh, trying to pretend to be cross—then staying us in all the frenetic energy, hand going to the heart she barely had, all pressing into her big boobs, her narrow little slumpy shoulders going slumpier as she played it up swoony-as, went on and on about that boy. When my sights were drawn elsewhere, she trailed off, and I saw how she had clocked the subtle little nod and held-in smile I made. She turned in time to see my Prefect giving me the exact same expression as she passed us. Rebecca swivelled back to me, shadows of disapproval in her brown eyes.

She had a long lanky kind of a face with mid-brown hair, a heavy fringe which poked about in her eyes, and I always thought she looked a bit like a horse. But not one I would want to ride. 'You're not still friendly with that girl?'

I shrugged, face going fire. 'Kind of.'

'Yeah, you are,' said Debbie. 'I've seen you the last three Saturdays in town with her. When you didn't come and meet *us*.'

'Duh. Big deal. I saw you too. And said hello.'

'You were holding her hand one time.'

'And...?'

'Well, you never do that with m—us.'

'I will if you want me to. Here,' I said, shifting my books to one hip, grabbing for her hand. She yelped, lurched back. I came after her, bigging up the bogeyman, all leering and grinning: come on, come on, little girl, give me your hand, type-thing. She was getting all high, shrieking and laughing as I chased her, Becca kind of tagging along, sort of squawking, the three of us running and weaving through the chaotic throng of kids.

'Girls!' We were cut up by that Miss George, the Home Economics teacher, a subject none of us took. She was stocky and stoic, was like she came out of a *Carry On* film, kind of like the Matron character, all boomy too, and we couldn't stop tittering as she arrested our shenanigans. 'Reign yourselves in, girls. Stop this silly behaviour. You're going to cause an accident.'

We skirted around her, Becca saying, 'Yes, Miss.'

'Hold up,' she instructed, so we all were forced to turn to her. 'You.'

'Me?' I said.

'Yes, you.' She beckoned with her finger. 'Come here. Where? Is? Your shirt?'

'My shirt?'

'*Miss*.'

'Miss.'

'*My shirt*, Miss,' she piped, all fluty.

'My shirt, Miss.'

'Well, where is it? Your shirt?'

'It's in my bag, Miss.'

'What's it doing in your bag?'

I shrugged.

'Well, go and put it back on. You know the rules. And get to your lessons, the three of you, or you'll be in deep trouble.'

The corridors were thinning now and as we quickly headed out of her view, bearing toward Blue House and our Geography class, I made a neighing sound with the word "Shi-i-i-rrrt", all whipping an imaginary switch at my own haunches. The hysterics we had been masking echoed about all over the place. I was always getting told off about not wearing my shirt under my V-neck jumper, but I liked the way it looked without it, all open and free. The sixth-formers were allowed to, and I didn't see why I shouldn't too. It was still school uniform. 'Hey,' I said. 'Why don't we bunk off? We're late now

53

anyway.'

'No way,' said Rebecca.

Debbie looked interested. 'Where would we go?'

'To town,' I ventured.

'No, because then I would have to miss German too and I'll never get away with it with Mr Saunders, he's a stickler.'

'You'll never get away with it with Mr Price either,' said Rebecca.

Debbie pulled in her slender lips, blew a sigh. 'She's right. You won't get away with it.' She fiddled with the mini tail at the nape of her neck, one little long bit sprouting from the shorn netherworlds of her haircut. She tutted. 'Oh…'

'Come on,' said Rebecca. 'We've got to go.'

I wrinkled my nose in a kind of sneer. 'See ya.'

'Where will you go?' Debbie was being yanked backwards as she spoke. I shrugged. 'See you later, yes?'

'Sure. I'll find you out front—at home time.'

'Are you going to skive your Art class too?' she called, falling into rhythm with her friend.

'Keep it down,' I hissed. 'No. Of course not.'

I spun back the way we had come, paused to check that crazed Home Economics teacher wasn't still around, slipped out the exit and down the paved path that led alongside Yellow House to Green House. The air was sharp and smelled of sulphur. They must have been doing some Chemistry experiment; I clocked them with their Bunsen burners and test tubes.

I went and put my folders into my locker and, on reaching the sixth-form common room, I paused, gathered my breath, entered about half-way, casual and natural-as. I scanned the space, saw how it was large and airy, had rows of uniform armchairs, Seventies ones with green-and-yellow cushions you could see the weave in, and skinny floaty wooden arms and legs, all lined up against the walls and under the big windows. There was a tea-making area, like a sort of breakfast bar. It looked pretty nice to be a sixth-former. She was nowhere about. I realised a couple of people were staring up at me from where they sat, just chatting, in their swish chairs, no work with them at all. 'Can I help you?' the girl said.

I shook my head, just kind of smiled, twirled myself back toward the door, beside which I caught sight of a KitKat vending machine. I fished in my skirt pocket, was pleased to find exactly twenty pee there in the form of the quite newly released twenty pence piece, my favourite now, of all the coins. I paused, relishing its snazzy seven-sided silver style, the rose with the crown on its "tails" side, as it sat there, all shiny in the palm of my hand. Inside my head, I said, Goodbye, sweet twenty pee, and inserted it into the slot, turned the lever, watched the KitKat plop into the dispenser.

There came a kind of shove from behind me. 'I'll have that.' The accent was high-pitched, sounded hard, like she came from East End London maybe. Her large arm barged me, snatched my chocolate bar.

'Hey,' I said, swivelling.

The KitKat was waving at me from this stocky girl's lean digits. 'You have no right to this.' She wore her thin fair hair scraped back in a low ponytail, her tan peg trousers ballooning beneath her loose-fitting shirt. You could see she was muscular—almost mannish, I thought—kind of attractive in the strangest, most repugnant way, her yellowish eyes all narrowed and giving me a beating.

I didn't try and grab my KitKat back, but I did hold her stare. 'I paid for it. It's mine, see.' Inside of me, I was bouncing around all over the place, didn't know what I was feeling.

'Ah.' She tore off the red-and-white paper wrapping, sliced her thumbnail through the foil between the two fingers of chocolate-covered wafer so I heard the tiny jingle of it.

I glanced to my right, scouted the room. No one was paying any attention. 'You can't—'

'—well, I am, aren't I?' She peeled the silver layer off of one side of the chocolate, snapped the fingers apart, bit into one, crunched joylessly. Her voice came in a low buzz and bits of biscuit on my cheek. '*You* have no right to this room *or* this machine, little *third*-former.' She stuck her pointing-finger into my chest. 'Now, get out. Or I'll be taking you down to the headmaster by your ear.'

'This isn't Dickens, you know.'

'Okay, now listen to me…' Her arm snaked around my shoulders, bodyweight manoeuvring me, with herself, out the door. She took me down the corridor quite a ways, polishing off my KitKat before rasping, her breath all chocolaty and delicious, 'As it happens, your timing is good. I've been wanting to have a quiet word with you for a couple of weeks now.'

'Hmmm?'

'Ya-ah.'

I attempted to pull myself out of her grasp, made muted noises of protest, but she gripped me in tighter. I felt the heat of her breath right in my ear. 'You're coming with me.'

'I don't want to.'

'Too bad.'

'What if I scream?'

'I don't think you will. What lesson are you supposed to be in? By the way?'

'I will eventually. If you do anything.'

'Well, I don't plan on hurting you—so long as you behave.'

'I won't behave.'

By this time we had reached the doorway to outside, and she

shoved me through with a sharp kick of her knee against my bottom. 'I think you will.' She hugged tight onto me as she walked me back past the science labs, me peering through the reflections to see if anyone was looking. I saw they were first-years anyway, recognising Katie Tippin's little sister from my village when she looked up and actually gave me a radiant wave.

As we travelled away from the school buildings, I realised we were entering the field that led to the railway station. The late-October wind billowed the long spindly grasses, went through the wool of my jersey; I felt the tension of the cold right into my jaw.

'I don't feel so comfortable going this far,' I said.

'Interesting.'

'What do you want from me?'

'Patience, my girl, is a virtue worth cultivating.'

I started to think maybe I should struggle out of her grasp, shout. My heart was all pounding in my ears. I made one incisive jerk. And the crook of her elbow tightened around my neck, full strength.

'I wouldn't if I were you.' Her tone cut through me.

My own voice came out as a shrill whisper. 'What are you going to do?'

'I told you, just a quiet chat.'

I couldn't help myself, my chest was starting to pant and heave and I understood I was trembling and tears were coming out of me. I just went all kind of weak and let her guide me wherever, all the world gone blurry and unreachable.

'Right,' she said, after some long minutes. And she flung me away from her, downward, so I teetered, crying out, and fell, the grass scratching at my bare knees, getting up under my pleats to bite my thighs.

All realising suddenly where I was, I felt a kind of rage, seemed to wake back into myself, and I stared up into her mean little yellows as if I meant to hit her myself. She couldn't hurt me. Even if she could.

'Recognise this?' She splayed open her arms, indicating the landscape.

'Yeh.'

'You were comfortable enough to come this far before, eh?'

'Yes.'

'So you know why we're here now?'

'You think I'm a—and you want to beat me up.'

She laughed.

'Well, I'm not.'

'You're not…what?'

'What you think I am.'

'Maybe. Maybe not. But either way, I want you to stop hanging about with—a *particular* girl.'

'What girl?'

'The one we're talking about.'

'Why should I? She's my friend.'

'Well, actually, she's *my* friend.'

'Oh?'

'And I don't want you messing with her anymore.'

'I see,' I said. I nodded in an assertive kind of a way, flashing some superior sense of myself at her. I brought myself to my feet. 'Yeah, I know who you are now.'

'She told you about me?'

'She did.'

'What did she say?'

'You should ask her. But you know, you can't own someone.'

'Whatever.' Her teeth clenched together, her hands making fists. Spittle into my face, breath gone acrid now, she told me, 'I'm telling you—I'm giving you a warning—keep the fuck away from her—'

'—or?'

Her fist flashed and thudded, the shock and the force causing me to buckle over, arms crossing over myself—*pain*—the realisation she had thumped me coming stark, and—I couldn't breathe—I couldn't find a way to suck in air—this pathetic raspy rattle just playing in my throat—my thoughts went black—the field fell away—and laughter—I could hear laughter—footsteps jolting towards—slaps on my back, between my shoulders—I sputtered—drew in a massive jerky breath, went all panty and gaspy—and *furious*.

I glared up at her through wet eyes, got the impression her eyes were wet too and I saw she was laughing and that was why, but I saw something else in there too, and I knew, somehow, in all of this, I held the power.

'I think you've got the message,' she said to me.

Not necessarily the one you want, I thought, as she turned and strode off, back up to the school buildings.

I sank onto my bum, all allowing the strange thudding pain she had imparted to just *be* in my body, feeling it spread and scream, the opposite of sparkles. I saw myself as a hero in a film. Maybe I'd been shot. Stabbed maybe. I let myself slump onto my back in the grass, gazing up at the pale-blue expanse with a few fried clouds in it. The sun-god put out his rays, lighting those clouds and stinging my eyes in a way that made me know I was alive. The ground had a dampness to it that seemed to soothe the scream. I remembered: This too shall pass. And I thought of my uncle and I wished I could see him. As if he spoke through me, I said, 'Now. I am now. I am here and now.' And I let the tingle of life spread through me, let myself be one with the sky and the earth and the bigness. I felt roused, felt my uncle guiding me, suggesting my big spirit-Self and little human me-self were merged, and this was the energy of Awareness-me, *now*.

I made it back in time for my Art class too, where we had to start a project inspired by Salvador Dali. I drew a picture of a melting girl, tucked it into my bag to make into a watercolour painting for homework. I went to meet Debbie and Rebecca out on the main entrance steps in the mass of excited yelling kids. The former's eyes lit when she saw me, the latter's looked disinterested.

'Where did you go?' Debbie said.

'Nowhere really.'

'Did you see your friend?'

My teeth came over my lower lip, containing my smile, eyes rolling back as I shook my head. 'I got beaten up.'

Debbie laughed.

'You know, you want to stop being so stupid and skipping class,' said Rebecca. 'And you want to stop telling lies.'

'Yeah, sure. What exactly are you getting at, Rebecca?'

'That you've turned into someone else lately. Ever since you slept in my bed with that stupid Robin Remick, you've been out to destroy yourself.'

'You really can be a cow, you know that? A bit dramatic, don't you think? Who said that—your mother?'

'Oh, and I saw your *lesbi*-friend. She went *that* way if you want to go and find her.'

Debbie gasped out loud, looked at me, eyes all wide, with her mouth pulled in.

'She's not...'

'I think she is actually—from what I've heard. And I don't know what that makes you?'

'What? I'm not—'

'—give it a rest. Seeing as you think everything's all natural and

60

that, I suppose you've done it with her too.' She shuddered, all embellished and mean-as.

'You know what, Rebecca? So what if I am. A lesbian. So what? You wanna go frig yourself—you need it. But I don't suppose you know how, huh?' I gave Debbie a bit of a twinkle, began a move toward the nestle of school coaches in the car park. 'I'm off. You two, play nice—or you want to come back to mine, Debs? My mum won't mind.'

'I—er—' the poor girl looked from me to the horsey-cow.

'She's invited back to mine,' said Rebecca, all smug. 'Actually. She's already staying over. Since yesterday.'

Debbie made indecipherable mumbles.

'Don't worry about it,' I told my silly friend.

'Well, I would like to but—'

'—I'll see you tomorrow, Debbie—if you're still talking to me, that is, after hanging around with this marvel of human creation and her delightful influence of a mother.'

Stink of an Unloved Flower

'Oh, and two liquorice shoelaces,' I said, pointing at the open plastic tub of skinny red strands all bunched together like a luxurious skein of wool.

Mr Hilary dipped his hand into the display case, and I watched him extract my request in his ancient hairy fingers, coax them into the little paper bag in which he had collected my other goodies. He smiled all kind of glowy, as if he understood my pleasure, his white-walnut skin rippling about like dry water. 'Anything else, dear?'

'Some toilet paper and—' I dug in my jeans' pocket, checking on the list my mum had given me.

'Over there, dearie,' he said, pointing behind me.

'—yes, three tins of tuna, a large tin of Chum and—oh, do you have any dark blue cotton?' I indicated my jeans. 'Like this?'

He bent, held up a reel of cotton all like it was my prize, and I smiled in thanks, went and got the other groceries myself, from the shelves. When I paid him out of my mum's money, he snuck me an extra Black Jack, saying, 'Don't tell the Mrs,' exactly as his portly ruby-faced wife came in from the back, and the two of them chuckled together, all flirty, the way they did whenever this sort of thing happened, which was all the time, for sure a game they were into. Feeling my unempathetic flush rush to mirror Mrs Hilary's rouge, I recalled how I used to laugh along when I was younger, get a welcome hit from their delight.

I put my head down, muttered, 'Thank you, Mr Hilary. Mrs Hilary. See you,' turned with my rattling white plastic bag, the loo paper tucked under my arm, to find myself face to face with a blushing Robin.

'Hey,' he said.

'Hey.' I stepped around him, my body instantly wavy, pounding, and made a dash for the outside.

'Hey, wait.' The sound of him was thumping after me. I wanted to run, fast as I could, I could have outrun him too, I knew it; I wanted to turn and yell the hell at him; I wanted to kiss him so badly. I slowed, my feet scraping on the rough surface of the narrow road but kept ambling. All shuddery in the winter cold, I let him come alongside me, my eyes rammed into the shiny black ribbon of pitch running the edge of the lane where the chippings hadn't reached when they had laid the tarmac. 'Do you want to…?' He pushed his shoulder into mine, so my body wheeled and my feet had to make up for it beneath me. His electricity surfed my cells. I kept my eyes down. 'You want to come sit in the church porch for a bit?'

My throat felt all tight and I found it hard to swallow. 'No thanks.'

'Aw. Come on…'

'I've got to get home.' I indicated the shopping, mortified by the realisation of the toilet roll I was showing him, this making me glance up, all side-eye, to check his reaction. He was looking intently at me, took the opportunity to keep my eye, swinging his own face around and under mine, all grinning so I saw his gappy teeth and the sheen of his skin and his polished brown eyes. He grabbed the handles of my plastic bag, his fingers boiling hot against mine cold. He tugged at it.

'Give,' he said, his breath flaring smoky in the frozen air. 'Give.'

I let go. Of the bag. Of the tightness in my chest. He twisted beneath me again and wrenched the toilet paper out from under other my arm, saying, 'This too,' sweet moist heat of him all into my face. He rammed the loo roll under his own arm. I let a smile puff out of me; just a crack of light allowed in. But I didn't give him my eyes. I kept those pinned to the trodden path of the grass verge we hopped up on as a car came, the stink of its exhaust perfuming the air like a bizarre unloved flower; I let him lead me away from my house, up the T-junction, to the hulk of flint-walled church above us.

As we passed through the open gateway, feet hitting the tamped earth with its litter of join-the-dots stones pressing up all like ribald faces, Robin Remick called out, and Tufty's white-blonde stringy basin-head loomed out of the porch, smiling large.

'There she is,' he said.

I smiled back, sucking on my lips, not sure if I was disappointed or relieved. But it was normal, really; Tufty was pretty much always hanging about the village with us—with Robin, essentially—and me—when I was with Robin. They even used to come down together to my uncle's stables and watch me train with him. The pair of them had been convinced I would become a jockey, just as I had myself, despite my mum and dad's insistence it was not even an option, and Robin especially, would kind of show off about it for me. Something of all of this flashed through my mind in the second it took for me to raise my hand in greeting. With this, an increased sense of how alone I had been lately. And an unexpected swell of affection for this hound-face friend.

'Tufty,' I said. 'Where've you been?'

He pulled his mouth down. 'Around. You?'

'Oh, the same. I haven't seen you once in…' I was going to say: "all this time"; maybe: "since that day at the garages"; "since September".

He picked up on my trail. 'A long while, eh?'

'Even though I pass your house just about every day.'

'Yeah…funny life,' he said, all kind of grown up. 'You seem to have got even taller. Is that possible?' A laugh flared through my nose, and I made a sharp nod. I didn't really like being tall then. 'You might even be taller than Robin now…' And he made us turn back-to-back, so he might check. 'Yup. You actually are, by an inch, I'd say.' And Robin Remick protested, playful-as.

The three of us crushed in through the arch of the small church porch, to sit on the built-in stone benches on either side. The stone was freezing under my bum. Tufty slid opposite me, allowing Robin Remick the choice. I could feel Tufty wanted things to be like they were before, and he didn't hide his pleasure when his friend slung himself up against me, finding excuses to hunch in close, rubbing his hands so they knocked against me, saying how cold it was, pincer-ing his fingers into my side so I wriggled, all tickled, all shrieking, like nothing had ever happened.

We fell into a rhythm of meeting up most days after school, wandering the village mostly, as was our want, until, several days before Christmas, I found myself entering Robin Remick's house with him alone. The holidays had started and Tufty had gone with his parents to visit his Nan in South End. My un-boyfriend lived also in a bungalow, but unlike Tufty's, his was a privately owned one, super-

Seventies, maybe five or six years old, all picture windows, built on a slope with a garden fanning out beneath it. In the summertime, Tufty and I would occasionally get to watch Robin Remick, all exerted, mowing that lawn.

With his mum at work, we entered the white-carpeted living room and flopped down, side by side, all shivery and awkward, on the wide white leather sofa. He flicked on the telly by the remote control. Everything Robin Remick's mum had was the latest—and giving-off-fancy in a show-offy kind of a way. I kind of liked it.

When a Fry's Turkish Delight advert came on, Robin openly crooned over the lush dark-skinned girl, and a hideous web of envy came latticing through my heart, creeping give-away rose into my cheeks. I leaned forward, elbows on knees, so he couldn't see me. Not that he was looking, I thought. The camera panned up her reclining body in her swishy belly-dancer silks, and I felt about ready to kill myself, watching as she opened her huge lustrous brown eyes beyond slowly, in close-up, gazed right into us. It was an impossible image I was to aspire to, in the deep dark secret of me, for a long time to come.

But Robin Remick fell away easily from her hook, stretched himself in a lean line, to fist a handful of red-skinned peanuts from a bowl on the gold-and-glass side-table.

'Do you want some?' he said.

I shook my head.

He filtered them into his mouth, all crunching and watching TV, sort of unconscious for a while, it seemed—until I got the feeling he was actually self-conscious and trying not to be. He shifted his legs quite a bit, sometimes brushing mine. He streamed more nuts between his full soft lips. And then, in a sudden lurch, making a clicky-sound with his tongue, he tossed a peanut in the air, sent himself skidding off the settee, all open-mouthed to catch it, snapping at it like Birdie when she dived for a treat. He looked to me, grin aglow. Cracked the nut between his teeth. I made a little guffaw, watched as he rolled around throwing peanuts up, lunging all over the place to catch them.

Panting and pretty pleased with himself, he nodded to the bowl. 'Come on. You chuck me one.'

'Me?' I reached, took a red-skin between finger and thumb, held it up, aimed. 'One. Two. *Three.*'

It soared across his living room and he followed its trajectory, landed it into the soft and warm of him, me going all squiffy inside, all girly in my giggles, plunging once more for the bowl, scraping up hard little nuts, all in a whizz-wheeeeeeee-wonder, targeting that portal, trilling as he caught each one. We were, the two of us, way up in the sky, laughing, eyes connected, sheened. I threw another. But he didn't go for this one, just let it arc and plummet; went, instead for me. He seemed to free-fall in slow-motion. And then he was grabbing my legs, my knees all into him, yanking me down into the thick soft carpet, sort of fighting me it felt like, hands into my waist, so I yelped and buckled and we were sliding about all over each other, like we must surely be a couple of seal pups, silky and smooth in the water, twisting and writhing, tumbling, turning and turning over one another. We were pressed together and the glory, the resonance, the wind and rain and sunshine all came crashing through me, almost winded me as he arrested the movement, threw me onto my back, clutched and held my wrists up over my head. He smiled right into me. Everything inside of me was jumping, puffing and bloating, expanding beyond my confines. His lips met mine, gentle, delicate-as. And my tongue plunged into his hot deliciousness and I found myself in the clearest blur as we played together, held each other in the long and many kisses. He made those butterflies on my throat, sent me into starlight oblivion. I kind of rolled him over so I sat astride him, nuzzled his neck as his hands massaged my boobs, looped over my bum in my skintight jeans.

He heard the car drawing up in his driveway before me. 'My mum,' he said, all pushing at me, pushing himself up onto his feet. 'Blast. She's early.'

We pulled at our clothes, pulled ourselves together, smoothed our hair, licked our own fingers over our faces, threw ourselves back into the settee. My heart was a speeding racehorse.

He took up the remote and flicked through the channels, went with that new soap-opera, Brookside, on the new Channel 4, let the remote sit super-casual in his lap, along with the peanut bowl. When his glamorous mother entered, all radiant brown complexion, black-as hair, jangling golden bracelets and dripping earrings, me and Robin Remick were chomping on the nuts.

I could tell she was surprised to see me. It was rare we went to each other's houses.

'Tufty not here?' she said, after greeting me, all friendly.

'Nah. He's away.'

'Do you want a cup of tea, you two?'

We both nodded. 'Yes, please,' I said. 'Would you like any help?'

'That's alright, angel.' She paused, frowned, looked at us, one to the other. 'You're looking quite hot, the both of you—I'll turn the heating down for you, shall I?'

I nodded, eyes sliding away, saw the white carpet was spattered with paper-fine peanut skins, felt a lurch to my heart, my eyes flicking back to hers.

'Do you take sugar?' she said, all easy.

I stood at Jimbo Clarke's front door wishing I didn't have to ring the bell—just kind of waiting, like perhaps this all might go away—when my wish came true, only not the way I meant, and the door was flung open, Jim's dad, arms akimbo, booming a hello. 'You made it. What a result that we bumped into you, huh? On your little shopping chore to Mr Hilary's the other week? Good comes of everything, my dear. You can't have Christmas without a party.'

Party? I thought. He insisted on taking my coat, which I wanted to keep on, and turned me into the kitchen doorway, all kind of proud, presented me to his wife. 'Come along, my dear,' he thrilled to me, his arm around my shoulder. 'Can't keep time waiting.'

He ushered me into the shadowy living room. The slight figure of Jim Clarke half-stood, sort of bowed even, from his pale-flowered armchair, little blue fishes all attentive, like he was from another time, and I got to feel like we were in some Jane Austin novel. I hoped he wasn't going to ask me to dance to the waltz-y music coming from the record player in the corner. He offered me the matching armchair opposite and as I sat, tugging my short denim skirt down as far as possible over my black woollen tights, he started to ask me something all kind of formal, like, was I having a good holiday?

His dad cut in, full-on blithe. 'Hold on,' placed a wooden side-table draped with a white lace-edged cloth between us, went and got the mince pies I had been invited to "partake in", and some sort of red drink with a clove floating in it. 'As promised.' He gave me a wink as he left us to it.

We chatted about nothing much. I nibbled on the edge of a mince pie, hand cupped under it, discovered the drink was a disgusting mulled wine I wouldn't be allowed at home. I kept thinking about that wink. Until this even worse image came, like we were some old couple destined to be married, holed up for eternity by the glowing coals of the fire, attended to by his smiley dad, who was the devil.

After a while Jim Clarke, looking all derogatory, brought up Robin Remick, telling me he'd seen him that same day I'd bumped into him and his dad.

A spark charged through me, all the way from my secret pink bud. 'What, just after you saw me? You sure it was that day?'

'Oh yeah, definitely.' His little fishes fired into mine. 'He was with that Tufty chum of—'

'—chum?' I said, a titter on my lips. I wanted to say, *Lashings of ginger beer!*

'That younger one he hangs around with, who goes to a different school.'

'I know who he is.'

'Of course.' He pulled in his lips, pustules blazing. 'Robin likes younger people, it seems. It must make him feel—what?—superior?—powerful? God-like maybe?'

'Jimbo. That's a bit—Tufty is a good—I like him too. But what, so you told them I was going to the shop then?'

'Yeh, I told him I'd just seen you on your way to pick up some shopping for your mum. I said you were doing really great.'

'Why did you tell him that?'

He twisted his mouth. 'I dunno. Shouldn't I have?'

I held my smile in with kissy lips.

'Shouldn't I have said?' he muttered again.

'It's fine. I just wondered why you mentioned me to him at all.'

70

'I dunno…I wanted him to know you don't need him. And I-I—yeah—I wanted to make him feel bad—the tosser.'

'Well…' I shrugged. 'I actually have to thank you.'

'Why?'

'He came and found me, see. At the shop. I wasn't sure if it was on purpose—but now I know it was.'

He frowned. 'He did? What did he say to you? I can't believe he would do that to you.'

'He didn't really say anything. But it's all gone back to normal and we've been meeting up all the time, Tufty too, of course. And…' My face was for sure shining.

'What?'

And then I felt kind of bad. I felt awkward. I wasn't so keen on the way Jim Clarke seemed to think I was his somehow. I wanted to just get up and leave but I couldn't yet, it would have been rude to his mum and dad.

'Nothing,' I said. 'I'm just glad all *that*—has passed.'

He swept up a mince pie, 'Hoof,' coming out of him as he jolted back in his armchair, fishes kind of flashing at me it felt. He bit hard into his cake and it crumbled, pieces of it scattering, breaking up some more as they tumbled down his stripy jersey, all dark bits of mince-stuff and yellow pastry. His old man hands brushed them away, sent them into his lap, into the cracks of the flowery armchair, where they were going to stick and for sure leave a mess.

I forced myself to eat. I asked him how the job was going for Rebecca's dad.

'I finished weeks ago.'

'Oh.'

'I heard you and Rebecca had a fight too.' He gulped on the horrible warm spicy wine.

71

I shrugged. 'Not really. I never liked her much anyway.'

'Yeah…' he said, sticking the remainder of his pie into his mouth. 'Well, you do seem to have pretty bad taste in friends.'

'Excuse *me*,' I said. 'What does that say about you?'

'You don't know who your friends are.'

I began to get up. 'Okay…know what? I'm going to—'

'—I mean, really, how can you be friends with someone who spread shitty rumours about you at school? Let alone still *like* him— by the looks of it? Don't you think that's embarrassing?'

'He *likes* me too,' I said, all plunging toward the exit. 'Actually.'

He huffed a laugh, said, 'Ha,' in a foul kind of a way, so I had to turn to see his fishes getting all beached in the scary wide whites he showed me. 'So you don't know?'

'What?'

'You seriously haven't heard?'

I wanted to say, Yeah, course I've heard. But I didn't have the foggiest what he was on about, and I felt a nasty kind of prickle on my skin and at the nape of my neck. I knew he could see I didn't know. The many swirls of the rug seemed to spring from my arrested feet all like a whirlpool, made me kind of stuck there.

Something flickered through his face that looked like vindication, but then I saw he felt sorry for me. 'You've been doing stuff with him, haven't you?'

'So?'

'Shit.'

'Why, because you—'

'—he has a *girlfriend*.'

'What?'

'At school. I can't believe you haven't heard. She's a second-year, was a friend of my little sister's. They've been seen snogging—all kinds of things—in a classroom. And she has love-bites all over her neck too.'

'Wha—' I was feeling I might lose my balance, my heart all swollen up, body spattering atoms, so parts of me were going missing '—oh god, no, I…oh god…I can't—wha—'

'—*what* have you been doing? You haven't gone and *done* it with him, have you?'

'No. No, I haven't done—what is this obsession with me doing *it*? It's none of your business anyway.'

'But you let him—*something*? Or what?'

'I-I didn't let him anything—I do what I want—oh, just get lost, will you, Jim, you prat, I—' I turned, shambled out the door, just about managed to say goodbye to his parents as they called out to me, managed to thank them and everything.

As I kept running, feeling myself exploding into pieces, tears and wails shattering out of me, I felt like I wasn't me and I was someone else: I was hearing and watching this girl turning her coltish legs beneath her, somehow keeping her footing as she stumbled about on the different surfaces she travelled, on the road and the pavement and the grassy verge, on the sticky mud of the shortcut, on the gravel of her own driveway, that sucked and tugged her nearly under. She was straining for breath when she slammed open the back door, fell into the kitchen, all wet and sticky with saliva and snot and sweat and tears. She hated Jimbo Clarke and she hated Robin Remick and Rebecca Hogarth and everyone.

'Hey, love!' It was my mum and she was coming after me as I drove myself, all gagging and spluttering, thumping up the stairs. I heard the commotion of the others downstairs, drawn by the drama of the girl that wasn't me. Someone from a film. Whose best friend had just died maybe. Or maybe it was she about to die herself. Yes, she was going to die.

I pitched this body onto my bed. My mum dived in, perched on the edge, her hand on me, rubbing me, saying all kinds of soothing kind things, just letting me, letting me…letting me. After some kind of eternity, she got me to sit up and she tweaked a tissue out from her sleeve and made me blow my nose in it whilst she was holding it, sort of pinching out my snot all like I was a little kiddie. And it felt pretty nice. I told her I hated mince pies and I never wanted to see one or smell one again. And what was that disgusting warm wine stuff?

'They gave you mulled wine?'

'They tried to,' I said.

One of her eyebrows went up. 'And you didn't like it?'

'Foul. Just foul. It shouldn't be allowed.'

She laughed and patted my leg with a whole lot of affection. 'My sweetheart. And you're sure you don't want to talk about it—what's going on? what happened?—you're sure?'

'I'm sure,' I mumbled, my cheeks feeling puffy and burning. 'Don't worry about it. I just over-reacted.'

'I've never heard you say that about yourself, my lovey.'

'I was just being silly.'

She chuckled some more, looked really sorry for me. 'Well if you change your mind…' She swept the dark lattice of hair from my face, peered in. 'Your uncle's here. He arrived just after you left. He can hardly wait to see you, lovey.' The thought of my uncle gave me to feel something almost lovely moving within me, like I was growing a dainty daisy in my heart. I saw how she saw this, and I liked that she did, and I felt it was possible I might grow a lawnful. 'So are you going to come down?'

I made a half-moon smile, breathed deep. 'I'll be down in five minutes, tell him.'

Entering my own living room, it was everything that boy's wasn't; it was love and ease and arguments that were safe, a place where everything always worked out, even the worst things and the mean things. The sappy wood in the fire in our grate snapped and popped, like it was delighted to see me. All the faces—my uncle, my mum, my dad, my dog, even my sister—gazed at me with a tender concern, and before my uncle could say anything, it was my sister asking, 'Are you okay?' and all mouthing, 'That Robin Remick git?'

The shock came to slap at me again, my chest blowing up inside, and I didn't know how I was going to wait to ask if she knew about the girlfriend and the love-bites and the snogging in the classroom.

I was being grabbed by my uncle, all crushed into his giant hug, enveloped by his fantastic expensive aftershave. He stepped back, holding me by both hands, his bald head all shiny in the incandescent light, eyes like pools you could swim in. My own eyes were rasping with tears again. He shook his head. 'Hey you.'

'Hey you,' I croaked.

'I've hit upon a tricky moment, huh?'

I shrugged, nose wrinkling, knuckled my eyes. 'I'm okay.'

'Sure. I know it.'

My mum rose, made a move toward the door, indicated to my sister. 'Come and help me with the potatoes, will you, pet?'

'And what about her?'

'Let's just give her a moment, don't you think?' To me, she said, 'You can do the dishes, lovey—yes?'

I gave a curt nod, biting on my lips, making pain there on purpose.

My dad was folding up his newspaper, flattening his hand over his greased-up hair, which was flat-as already. 'Have I got time for a quick cycle around the loop?'

'Yes, there's lots of time,' my mother said. 'You can even go around the North Circular, if you want to.'

No one laughed and my sister dug the jab in. 'That's not funny, Mum.'

'I'll nip upstairs and get changed, then,' my dad murmured, as he sluiced his lengthy form through us, chest kind of concave. He patted my shoulder, hard, the way he did, said, 'You'll be okay, love.' And up came this crazy image of him whizzing on his racing bike all round the ring road about a hundred of miles away, zooming around Central London in his professional Lycra cycling gear, all lanky and like a cartoon, and I thought it actually *was* funny and I began laughing a bit, all juddery, which made my tears come sprouting out.

As they all left the room, my uncle said, 'Come and sit,' guided me to the settee with him. I grabbed for his hands, twisted them, so I could see the ragged self-made tattoos on the backs of his lower phalanges. It was something I had done since I was a little girl, when I used to climb onto his lap, which I kind of wished I could right now. My voice came stuck in my throat. 'You've still got them.'

He smiled, nodded in a wry sort of a way. 'They're not going anywhere.'

I read one out: H A T E

He read out the other: L O V E

'Which is it?'

'You tell me, my love...'

'I don't know. Both, maybe. Can you love someone and hate them at the same time?'

'Yeah...but—'

'—don't be telling me the hate is an illusion.'

'Well...it is, isn't—'

'—but then the love is an illusion too.'

'No. The love is the essence of all things. The hate is simply

76

Love's shadow, and thus they live in close proximity. Yin and yang. Hate—throws light on Love, makes love brighter, no? Shows you Love is your answer. When you turn on the light you discover the dark doesn't exist.'

I knew he would go into all of this, and truth is, I wanted him to. However much I didn't. 'Ah, but you can't say an actual shadow is an illusion. It's as real as the thing, see.'

'But you can say the thing is an illusion.'

'*Every*thing is an illusion, you say. Me—my self—my body—I mean, nothing actually exists as far as you're concerned.'

'It's the way we project onto reality—and identify—as if it is the ultimate truth, that creates the illusion, my darling—thus every *thing* becomes a construct, a projection of the mind. But energy exists— and pervades everything, huh? Therefore you exist. In the form of Consciousness. You could say love is Consciousness—'

'—no, *you* could say that.'

He raised his eyebrows, laughing in a puff through his nose. 'I will say: Love is, in its essence, the state of silent aware energy. Which is pouring into and through all life, *experiencing* life—through you. It doesn't get better than that.'

'But if our life is an illusion?' I held out my hands. 'Why? All of this? This life and everything? This life that hurts and burns and scars? What's the *point*?'

'Maybe, the point is…there is no point.'

'Duh. Do you even know what you're talking about? Really?'

He chuckled. 'Do any of us? When it comes to it? Isn't life itself the point—the experience of joy—and of pain, this shadow, this hate? A coming to one's Self, through this? The thirteenth century Zen master, Dogan, tells us: "To study the Buddha way is—'

'—noooooooo—' I made a crucifix of my forefingers '—not your blasphemous Buddha—' acting all missionary Christian '—no, please—'

'—to study the Buddha way is to know the self—to study the self is to forget the self—to forget the self is to be enlightened by the ten thousand things." The eternal mysteries of Being, dear lovely, no?'

'You are way too intense. Do you know how old I am?'

'You are an old soul, little one. Hear: "mysteries". Enjoy them. These things take time. A lifetime. And more. I'm always still learning myself. We just have to fall in love with discovering our true nature—*through* the reflection pain offers us—it's the ultimate devotion, my lovely.'

'Euggh...bog off—devotion schmotion—who cares?'

'Okay, perhaps it is by feeling the hate, the dark—which you are *not*—you get to realise yourself for what you truly are.' He paused, eyes soft, wide open. 'Are you having boy trouble?'

I gave a vague nod. Then, referring to his tattoos, I said, 'How old were you again?'

'Well, finally I can say: about your age. Now you're this age.'

I smiled, gratified with this answer. 'With the biro you broke open and the compass?' I loved this story, knew all the answers. I had the feeling inside of me almost as if the tattoos were mine and I had scored them into his fingers myself, seen the bright blood spring, blue all mixing in.

'And who is this unenlightened fellow, who doesn't see your brilliance?'

'Just an idiot really. I've realised. He's not worth it.'

His eyebrows were raised, and he breathed a laugh, as if maybe he didn't believe me. 'He *really* isn't worth it. You know that?'

'I know. I know.' I eyeballed him. '*And* my pain is an illusion.'

He made a playful victorious laugh. 'You are one fine study.'

'And I'm doing it to myself...clinging to the pain, huh? What is it you say? Re-creating suffering with my mind, so it happens again and again and again? Oh, I *see*—equals, illusion.'

'Okay, your tone is a little—this is not meant as a self-flagellation. I'm not saying your pain isn't real, in this life experience, and that it doesn't matter. Just, you express it, allow it through, then you let it go. When you can. You observe, hold an awareness, *kindly*. And you grow.'

'Pig,' I said. 'Easy to say. Sometimes I just hate being me, see.'

'Ah.' He gazed at me, and I saw how he totally got it—got *me*.

'Yes—' I said '—hey, but I really am realising—um—I don't know—quite a lot, see? I suppose. It just might take a while to—see?—stop loving him—and stop hating him too, see. Maybe it's good if hate is an illusion.'

He was nodding. 'The quality, the *tone*, of love can change, my lovely. I hope you will love him always.'

'That's kind of messed up—I really hope not. But I suppose I sort of kind of know what you mean. Kind of. If I have to.'

'There's my girl,' he said.

'Yeah…here I am.'

He held me tight in those pools of his, so it really did feel I might be able to get through all of this. 'I'm thinking…' he said. 'You're missing the horses, right?'

'Yeah…' My energy sort of grated. 'It really is kind of unbearable sometimes.'

'Well, why don't you come for a visit? How about Easter? You can help with the training and everything. We have a beautiful practice track. And my new lead trainer—man, he's phenomenal—he'll teach you a lot; I'd love you to work with him. He's worth his weight in gold—and he's going to see you are too, with all your intuitive understanding and spooky ability to guide the horses.'

'Ye-ahhhhh.' My arms flew themselves around his neck. 'Yes.'

'Fantastic, it's settled then. I've already arranged it with your mother—as it happens.'

'You did? She said yes? Wheeee! Brilliant. Ireland: here I come.'

'We'll have a ball, all of us.' He gave me a nudge. *'Now…'* I nodded in anticipation of what I knew was coming. 'Being *now.* Shall we…?' I grinned, sat myself upright. 'Okay…settle yourself. Just feel into yourself and begin to recognise your energy. Your fundamental life force, yes? Pure energy: the Love you, huh? You feel the tingle?' I nodded ever so slightly. 'In your hands?'

'Yep.'

'In your head and neck? Up your spine? You feel the silence, huh? The ease—the stillness beneath the world of form? This is You, my little sweet. You are this simple Awareness. Pure unconditional Love. How good does that feel, eh?'

'Mmmm…'

'You with You. This is it, my lovely. You are Life. You are a unique expression of Love, of Spirit. Do you see?'

I opened my eyes, feeling all light and jusshy, my body bouncing in its glory, all expanding out of itself—without a boy or a girl or a kiss or anything. Laughter ran out of me. 'You're a magician,' I told him. 'A terrible, *bad* magician.'

'You: here and now; somewhat clarified. Until the next bugger comes along, eh, my love?'

I shook my head. 'There won't be a next one.'

'Of course not,' he said.

We gazed at one another for a long sunlit moment, and then, easy-as, all joy and knowing, we were laughing.

Printed in Great Britain
by Amazon

77332510R00053